On the physical plane, their mouths touched, their breath mingled, and Macklin teased the seam of Jordan's lips gently with his tongue.

Behind Macklin's eyes, things were even more exciting than that. Fireworks, crashing waves, a hurricane of breathless longing: all of it made his palms tingle to touch more, made him want to plunder.

"Do we?" Macklin asked, his breath coming quicker.

"Want more?" Jordan asked, sounding equally as breathless.

DREAMSPUN BEYOND

Dear Reader,

Love is the dream. It dazzles us, makes us stronger, and brings us to our knees. Dreamspun Desires tell stories of love featuring your favorite heartwarming heroes, captivating plots, and exotic locations. Stories that make your breath catch and your imagination soar.

In the pages of these wonderful love stories, readers can escape to a world where love conquers all, the tenderness of a first kiss sweeps you away, and your heart pounds at the sight of the one you love.

When you put it all together, you find romance in its truest form.

Love always finds a way.

Elizabeth North

Executive Director
Dreamspinner Press

Amy Lane

PENTACLES AND PELTING PLANTS

DREAMSPUN
BEYOND

PUBLISHED BY
DREAMSPINNER
PRESS

Published by
DREAMSPINNER PRESS

5032 Capital Circle SW, Suite 2, PMB# 279,
Tallahassee, FL 32305-7886 USA
www.dreamspinnerpress.com
This is a work of fiction. Names, characters, places, and incidents either
are the product of author imagination or are used fictitiously, and any
resemblance to actual persons, living or dead, business establishments,
events, or locales is entirely coincidental.

Pentacles and Pelting Plants
© 2021 Amy Lane

Cover Art
© 2021 L.C. Chase
http://www.lcchase.com
Cover content is for illustrative purposes only and any person depicted
on the cover is a model.

Paperback ISBN: 978-1-64405-940-1
Digital ISBN: 978-1-64405-939-5
Paperback published October 2021
v. 1.0

Printed in the United States of America
∞
This paper meets the requirements of
ANSI/NISO Z39.48-1992 (Permanence of Paper).

Award winning author **AMY LANE** lives in a crumbling crapmansion with a couple of teenagers, a passel of furbabies, and a bemused spouse. She has too damned much yarn, a penchant for action-adventure movies, and a need to know that somewhere in all the pain is a story of Wuv, Twu Wuv, which she continues to believe in to this day! She writes contemporary romance, paranormal romance, urban fantasy, and romantic suspense, teaches the occasional writing class, and likes to pretend her very simple life is as exciting as the lives of the people who live in her head. She'll also tell you that sacrifices, large and small, are worth the urge to write.

Website: www.greenshill.com
Blog: www.writerslane.blogspot.com
Email: amylane@greenshill.com
Facebook: www.facebook.com/amy.lane.167
Twitter: @amymaclane

By Amy Lane

DREAMSPUN BEYOND
HEDGE WITCHES LONELY HEARTS CLUB
Shortbread and Shadows
Portals and Puppy Dogs
Pentacles and Pelting Plants

DREAMSPUN DESIRES
THE MANNIES
The Virgin Manny
Manny Get Your Guy
Stand by Your Manny
A Fool and His Manny

SEARCH AND RESCUE
Warm Heart
Silent Heart
Safe Heart
Hidden Heart

Published by **DREAMSPINNER PRESS**
www.dreamspinnerpress.com

To my reader's group—Amy Lane Anonymous—for keeping my spirits up when I was writing. And to my Mate, who still loves me. And to my dogs, who think I'm tits.

Acknowledgments

THANK you, Mary, for being my Wiccan consult, and never once saying to me, as Dan Aykroyd said to Bill Murray, "You never studied."

Author's Note

FOR the record I own about six zillion books on witchcraft, and my computer has been some very interesting places. I've read books about flowers and books about candles and books about herbs, and what it all comes down to, and the reason I can't remember a damned thing from any of that research, is human intent. Intend kindness and follow through. Intend honesty and follow through. It's the greatest witchcraft humans know.

Help!

BANG! *Bang! Bang!*

With every fist against the door, a trail of rainbow sparkles exploded on the other side. Jordan and the little group of hedge witches who had put out an SOS that night jumped with every burst of color, and Jordan leapt to his feet.

Oh Goddess. Please let this be help.

Almost three weeks ago—had it only been three weeks?—Jordan and his old college friends, his little coven of seven, including himself, had gotten together after too much wine (on his part) and too much self-pity (well, on everybody's part) and cast a spell for their hearts' desires.

And then they had all, every damned one of them, apparently lied their asses off about what it was they really wanted.

And the magic had gotten pissed off. Like, *vindictive-as-fuck* kind of pissed off. The little cul-de-sac where Jordan and his friends lived had gone straight to hell—quite literally. Birds flew upside down, squirrels marched ad infinitum, and snakes hung from the apple tree.

The cul-de-sac itself consisted of three newer houses—two bedroom, ranch-style one-story, just-starting-out houses with cream-colored stucco and green trim that looked as average as any stucco cul-de-sac house ever looked—and one ramshackle witch's cottage, with peeling paint and a crooked roof and nine feline familiars who guarded the place from vermin and, apparently, the anger of the magic itself, because as far as Jordan could tell, the cats were the only reason the cottage hadn't simply imploded.

Jordan had been forced to live in the damned witch's cottage ever since the witch herself had *bailed* on it, leaving Jordan and his friends in charge of her home, her magical library, her self-cleaning cat-box sandpit in the back, and her giant wall of medicinal and essential oils that Jordan was absolutely not allowed to touch but that he and his friends had tried hard to emulate.

Because as soon as the witch had taken off, thrusting her keys into Jordan's hands and basically riding off into the sunset on her little motorcycle, Jordan and his friends had taken over the idea of creating magic.

And it had been great—truly great. They all had their specialties. Jordan was a scientist, an entomologist, and he was good at distilling the essential oils that they used in many of their spells. His right-hand man was Bartholomew Baker, who worked IT for money but whose true magic was as, well, a baker. He could bake magic cookies that calmed the most fractious heart or assemble the ingredients of an airtight protection spell without much more than good intentions and a dreamy intensity. Alex—Barty's roommate—wasn't as powerful a witch, but he was very good at keeping the rest of them organized and on task, and that was a special magic all its own.

Dante, a journalist who seemed to be constantly seeking his own creative space, was their wordsmith for spells. His roommate, Cully, who was a costume designer, was particularly good at finding the way for the physical parts of a spell, including colored threads and their meanings, to weave together. Kate and her boyfriend, Josh, who were two of the kindest, most empathetic people Jordan had ever met, rounded out their little group, and they were good at substitutions and figuring out the main ideas. Did a spell call for anise for sweetness when it seemed the numbing properties would be counterintuitive? Kate would suggest cinnamon instead, and the spell would become perfect.

Together the seven of them had done good things, kind things. From Bartholomew's magic cookies that calmed traumatized children to Cully's little sachets, filled by Kate and Josh, that eased a colleague's heartbreak, Jordan believed their coven was a wholesome part of their community, something valuable that generated kindness and affection and a sort of sweetness he saw in his college friends that he thought was underappreciated in the world.

Right up until that damned heart's desire spell had sent their neighborhood tumbling into cartoon hell—and had literally swallowed two of his friends.

Dante and Cully, roommates, guys who should have been lovers since college but who had routinely missed each other because *they* were the only thing that the two of them were stupid about, had walked into their house and gotten lost in time. They could be seen, talked to, heard—but not at the same time. One of them would talk to whoever was visiting and then walk through a wall and disappear. The other would call through the door, but when somebody walked into the house, his voice could still be heard even though he'd be out of sight.

And if Jordan and his friends didn't perform a ritual at sunrise and sunset every day, on the dot, the weirdness of their cul-de-sac threatened to spill out into the adjoining neighborhoods.

Jordan was legitimately terrified that not only would Dante and Cully be lost to them forever, but their entire town would be swallowed by the hell dimension fighting to take over their cul-de-sac.

The remaining five witches had been honestly at their wit's end before Alex's boss—and new boyfriend—had suggested that the lot of them send out a help signal to the forces that be.

They'd performed the spell a few days later, seven chants of "Help us in our need!" going out, with a different rainbow sparkle shooting out of the cone of power with every chant. The cone was formed when they joined their hands and performed their rituals, and Jordan knew he wasn't the only one who had poured his whole heart into making their rescue beacon as strong and heartfelt as possible.

He and his friends were *sorry* they'd screwed up so incredibly badly.

Please, please, all they wanted was someone to tell them how to fix things and make amends.

So the pounding on Bartholomew and Alex's door in the middle of the night was more than anticipated. It was welcome.

But that didn't prevent Jordan from experiencing a frisson of fear as he went to open the door.

The man waiting in the doorway was not what he'd expected.

Midthirties, six feet or so to Jordan's six feet five inches, he had a two-day's growth of black beard over a square jaw, wild black hair with the occasional gray hair twisted through it, a battered leather jacket, and the most piercing blue eyes Jordan had ever seen.

"Hi, uh—"

"Who in the *fuck* sent that goddamned portal?" their new guest demanded, sweeping into Alex and Bartholomew's living room in a swirl of fury and cold wind and leather.

"A what?"

"A portal!" The stranger sounded aggrieved, and on closer inspection, he looked, well, tired. "A portal that grabbed me by the scruff of the neck and sent me hundreds of miles from my location to where I could see a signal that practically screamed my name!"

"Oh. Sorry," Jordan began, his hackles rising immediately. Oh *fuck* this. He and his friends could do this on their *own* goddamned time!

"And who in the *fuck* sent this neighborhood to hell?"

"Oh!" Josh said, and Jordan glanced at him as his big guileless brown eyes lit up in sudden understanding.

"That's what happened, isn't it? Like, that's literally what happened?"

Josh's girlfriend patted his shoulder, and Jordan turned to the belligerent stranger to answer for his coven's mistakes.

"That would be—" he began again.

"What in the hell is happening here, and who in the fuck is in charge?" their savior demanded.

"Well, if you would shut up for a fucking minute, I'd tell you!" Jordan snapped. "Jesus, do you always talk this much? Would you land on the fucking *Titanic* and bitch about the goddamned ice, or would you throw those poor people a raft?"

Alex—small, green-eyed, ginger-haired, and pragmatic to the bone—slid in behind their new guest and shut the door before Dante and Cully's bichon frise, Glinda, could escape, and while Jordan noted the move and nodded thanks, their new guest didn't even blink.

"I assume you were asking for my help!" Leather Jacket and Attitude snarled. "Was I mistaken?"

"Well, you were asking questions. I *assumed* you wanted answers. My name is Jordan Bryne, and this is my coven—*most* of my coven—and yes, we need help. Are you going to hit us? Shoot us? Scream at us? I warn you, I'll hit, shoot, or scream back, but most of us are sort of gentle people, and you'll end up with a bunch of angry, resentful hedge witches who won't tell you *shit*. If you would stop yelling, maybe we could have us a conversation!"

Their new savior's eyes narrowed. "Hedge witches?" he asked, sounding doubtful. "This amount of damage was done by hedge witches? Who's your wizard? Your grand witch? Who owns the cottage on the corner? Someone had to put a lot of power into that beacon, because portals take a hell of a lot of power!"

Alex frowned. "We put the signal out at sunset, and it's 2:00 a.m. now. What took you so long?"

The newcomer gave him a level look. "It didn't zap me *here*—it zapped me *near* here," he said without blinking.

Alex gave a self-conscious laugh. "Yeah, sorry. We did something like that to the dog this last week. My bad. I totally see how that could happen. Carry on, uh… whoever you are. Barty, did he mention his name?"

Bartholomew Baker, with sandy brown hair and enormous gray eyes, was the shyest, most introverted person in the coven—and possibly Northern California. He shook his head. "No. No, he didn't. He's trying to bully us. Bullies don't give names."

And that brought the newcomer up short. He stared at Bartholomew. His mouth parted slightly, the fearsome *V* that had creased his forehead eased up, and those blue eyes lost some of their crackle, if none of their intensity.

"I'm not trying to bully you," he corrected, but Bartholomew gave him a mutinous, wounded glance, and he apparently rethought himself. "My name," he went on, "is Macklin Quintero. I'm a wizard, born into a family of wizards, the third son of a third son of wizards, and in my entire life, I have never, ever seen a neighborhood like yours. What *happened* here?"

Jordan's anger died a quick death, but only because Macklin had backed off Bartholomew.

"If you'll sit down," he said, trying hard to be courteous, "here, at this table, we can get you something to eat or drink and introduce ourselves and tell you. We've been trying to fix it for three weeks, and we could really use your help."

Macklin's mouth twisted up in what seemed like it was going to be a sneer, but Jordan cut him off.

"But we'll kick you out if you want to be a dick about it, because you know what? Nobody craps on my coven. I don't care if you piss lightning and shit frogs. Whatever your credentials, if you're not here to help us shove this genie back in the bottle, you are not welcome. *Particularly* if you're going to be a dick."

Macklin took a step back and cast a reassessing glance around the room. Everybody was standing up, staring at him with hard eyes—even the dog, who was, for the first time in Jordan's experience, growling.

"Et tu, Brute?" Macklin asked Glinda.

Glinda showed him her teeth.

He cracked a half smile and glanced around the room again. "Okay," he said. "Fine. Thank you for the offer of food and drink. I'm sorry I was a…." He grimaced at Jordan. "A dick." He let out a breath and his shoulders sagged and some of his attitude bled out. "I was on a motorcycle ride through Nevada when your summons ripped me through a portal and put me halfway here. I don't know which one of you is full-tilt wizard here, but I'm telling you people, this was *not* the work of hedge witches having a little fun."

"Well, that's what we were," Jordan said, his shoulders relaxing a little. "Would you care to sit down? Barty made cookies. Believe me, if you think a portal was magic, that's because you haven't tasted his chocolate oatmeal raisin."

Macklin raised his eyebrows. "Wow. Okay. Fine. The couch is fine—"

"*The table!*" they all said in concert.

Macklin's gaze slid to the table, and his eyebrows hit his hairline, bounced a couple of times, and came to rest about halfway up his forehead. "Okay," he said, letting out a breath. "Somebody, *somebody*, has *got* to tell me what in the fuck is going on."

Heartaches by the Number

MACKLIN eyed the table, getting a better look at it, and raised his eyebrows again. It was… well, unusual. It wasn't often that people incorporated skilled woodwork and intricate spell crafting. He had to give kudos to whoever had put this together.

The table itself sat seven, which was a tough thing to do because a heptagram is by nature asymmetrical. But it was a seven-sided, beautifully finished piece of maple wood, with corners beveled and sanded smooth. Inlaid in the center was a spectacular design: a black rainbow sun, its center swirling with sparkles and mystery and its different colored "rays" reaching out like numbers on a clock.

He held his hands over the matte-burnished surface, glanced at Jordan Bryne of the ice-blue eyes and transparently blond eyebrows, and tilted his head. "Binding?" he asked.

"There's nothing binding," Jordan said. "And it doesn't compel you to do anything. But it does let you know if someone at the table isn't being truthful, and that's why we want you to sit there."

"So you know if I'm lying?" he asked, approving very much. They'd all seemed so lost in the rain. This, at last, smacked of some savvy.

"So you know if we are," Jordan told him, cocking one of those eyebrows. His entire face, from the pale golden hair to the knife-edged Scandinavian cheekbones, spoke of a sort of aristocratic poise that Macklin resented to his very bones.

But then Jordan went and said something like that—something so innocent that Mack normally would have patted the man on the head and walked away—and Macklin was leveled, caught, sucked into whatever fairy tale these sweet little college kids had spun out of fancy and some scented oils.

Macklin smirked. "I'd know if you were lying."

And it was Jordan's turn to tilt his head. "Really?" he asked mildly. "*We* didn't. And that's how this whole thing started."

Macklin knew his eyes went wide. "O-kay…. What did you lie about? Did somebody plant the wrong roses in the backyard? Someone use bleach instead of enzymes in their laundry? I'm dying to know what sort of fib caused this entire neighborhood—"

"Cul-de-sac," Jordan corrected, voice steely. "I assure you, if we hadn't been working our asses off to keep this contained, it would *be* the neighborhood, but now it's the cul-de-sac. And sit down at the table, let us get you some food and some drink, and let's be pleasant

to each other. We asked you for help. Let us show you
some hospitality first."

Mack had to take a deep breath at that. He'd
stormed into this pleasant little house with people
who'd asked him for help and assumed that he was
working with fools or assholes. The idea that the
portal that had dragged him halfway here—and the
pull of magic that had made it impossible to stop the
journey when he'd been plopped in the middle of I-80
going 60 mph—had been inadvertent hadn't even
crossed his mind.

"Thank you," he said slowly, allowing himself
to sink down into a padded wooden chair. The chairs
were from a different dining room set—something
more commercial—but the table.... Wow, that was a
work of art. He closed his eyes and held his hands over
it, feeling the buzz of many different kinds of magic
singing in harmony through the wood.

"Where did this come from?" he breathed, a child
in his wizard's workshop all over again. For a moment
he could smell sage, cedar, vetiver, lavender, rue, pine
sawdust, and leather. And he could feel the lash of his
father's tongue as well.

"That's complicated," Jordan said. "Barty—that's
Bartholomew of the enchanted cookies," Jordan said,
indicating the fair young man with the enormous gray
eyes. "His boyfriend, Lachlan—"

"Ginormous boyfriend," corrected the lone woman
in the room.

"*Ginormous* boyfriend, Lachlan," Jordan echoed
with a slight smile. "Lachlan made the table, but the
rest of us here—Alex," he indicated the compact
ginger-haired man by the door, "myself, Kate," he gave
a nod to the curvy young woman, "and her boyfriend,

Josh, were the ones who cast the spell that really amped up the power." Josh, a hulking, muscular man with a cheerful grin, raised his hand in acknowledgment.

"Yeah, well, Lachlan was sort of pissed at us when he made the table," Kate said dryly. "Jordan, sit. I'll get snacks ready. It's my turn."

"I'll help," Bartholomew said, sidling past Macklin warily, and Macklin wanted to bang his head against this absolutely beautiful table.

"Is Lachlan a witch?" Macklin asked. "Why isn't he here?"

"Well, he's got power we didn't know about," Jordan said. "Which only makes sense because we didn't realize how powerful Bartholomew was until he met Lachlan. So yes, some of this is his doing. The eternity circle in the middle, though, like I said, that's Alex, Barty, Kate, Josh, and me. We don't know if it has any powers yet—"

"It does," Mack assured him. "How did it get there?"

"That," Jordan said, mouth quirked grimly, "was our last spell."

Mack blinked, impressed. "Well done!"

Alex made a noise between a snort and a sob.

"That was not what we were trying to do," Jordan said, nodding at Alex before gesturing with his chin for him to sit down.

Alex sat wearily next to Jordan and gave his friend a small smile.

"The spell unleashed a lot of power," Alex said. "And it did get *something* done. But we were trying to fix this mess, and quite obviously we failed."

Reluctantly, Mack felt for the young man. "Well, the result is very pretty," he said, feeling like a heel.

"Thank you," Alex said, but his disheartenment was quite clear.

"Are there only five of you?" he asked. "Where's the guy who built the table?"

"Home," Jordan said, giving Bartholomew a quick glance. "There were, originally, seven of us. In the last three weeks, we've added a couple of people—"

"So, nine," Macklin said, but Jordan, Kate, and Josh all shook their heads.

"Here," Jordan said. "It'll help if you listen to us from beginning to end. But first, everybody come touch the table. He needs to know if I'm telling the truth, because that would cut out a whole lot of 'are you kidding me' that I sense coming."

Bartholomew set a board with cheese and meat, neatly sliced, on the table, and Kate added a basket of bread and another one full of cookies. Her significant other put a bowl of sliced apples down, along with a small stack of plates. The motions were very… coordinated. These were people who broke bread together often.

"Oh, wait!" Bartholomew hopped up and trotted to the hugely modern—and obviously refurbished— kitchen and returned with butter, a butter knife, and some crackers for the cheese-and-meat plate. He set everything down and took stock of the table setting, then looked at the woman who'd helped him. "Is that everything, Kate? You think?"

Kate chuckled and leaned her head on his shoulder for a moment. "Sweetheart, it's after two in the morning. You just pulled appetizers out of your ass in the wee hours. If he's too dumb to appreciate you, we're not."

Bartholomew's smile at his friend was sweet and soft and sugary, and Mack almost held his hand to his heart. Who *were* these people?

"Josh, sit down." Jordan gestured, pointing to the chair next to Alex. The placement put Jordan at one end of the table and Mack at the other, and the significance wasn't lost on Mack.

He'd come in all swagger and irritation, and he'd set himself at odds with this little coven. Fantastic. *Shades of the old man, Macklin. Dammit! These aren't wizards. They're decent people. Fuck.*

"So, I'm going to start off telling a lie," Jordan said. "Keep your hands on the table and you'll see what happens. My name is Jordan Bryne, and my mother and father are happily married and living in Grass Valley."

"Ouch!" The jolt of electricity that traveled up Macklin's hands and into his arms practically numbed his wrists. "Dammit! That smarts. Your parents must *really* hate each other!"

Jordan gave a mean chuckle. "They actually get along okay, as long as they live in different counties. My father lives with his husband in Grass Valley. It's very prime-time TV."

Macklin felt a tingle along his fingertips and frowned. "There's more to it than that," he murmured.

Jordan sighed. "My mother's been a recovering addict for eighteen years," he said. "She lives in another county because her NA group is there, and she needs them. But the rest was true—sorry, it was a lie by omission, which I guess shows you how powerful this table really is."

Macklin nodded, looking at the table—and at Jordan—with respect. He'd chosen a personal secret to tell, an uncomfortable one, and he'd done it on purpose. Macklin understood now that even if the things the group told him seemed like oversharing, they were doing it for a reason.

"Got it," he said quietly. "My name, as I said, is Macklin Quintero, and I am so very proud of my behavior when I walked into your house a few moments ago."

He saw Jordan wince before he was done speaking, and everybody else jerked their hands away from the wooden surface, apparently anticipating where that statement was heading. Jordan kept his hands planted, though, and shuddered as the zap passed through him.

He sucked air in through his teeth for a moment and shook out his arms and hands when it was over. "Apology accepted," he said, a bit of grim amusement quirking at his eyebrows.

Mack nodded, confirming that had been his intention, and for a moment, they regarded each other steadily over the table.

And Mack had to swallow against the sudden tug of attraction zinging through his bloodstream. Damn, those arctic blue eyes and his lean, sculpted mouth. Add in a long jaw and blond hair that had probably been dark during childhood, and Mack realized that his pansexual attraction meter had been pinging since he'd stalked into the modest little home.

Jordan broke eye contact first, a red crescent appearing on each high cheekbone, and Mack knew he wasn't alone.

Well, thank God for that.

"So I get it," Mack said, reaching for a small plate. "What you guys are going to tell me is the truth and not bullshit. And you're willing to feed me and, I assume, let me sleep on somebody's couch so we can try to fix this. I'm game. You guys talk, I'll eat."

Jordan sighed and picked up a slice of what appeared to be homemade bread from the basket and slathered some butter on it. He took a bite and closed his eyes before nodding at Bartholomew appreciatively. "Good job, Barty," he praised, and his very shy friend ducked his head and smiled.

"Okay," Jordan said. "It all started when my crush at work told me she was dating my other crush at work, and he'd asked her if they could invite me into a threesome."

Mack's eyes were going to dry out, so he blinked—a lot. "That's a problem?" he asked to make sure.

Jordan glanced at his friends in a little bit of embarrassment. "Well, it might not have been, except they were *crushes*," he said. "I… I cared about them. I couldn't, you know, yell yippee and dive into bed. It's not how I'm wired."

Macklin nodded, liking that response, dammit. "Understood," he said, and he could tell by the flags of color that only grew brighter on Jordan's cheeks that this wasn't easy for him to tell somebody outside of his little circle.

"So I came home, drank too much wine—"

"Like you do," Macklin agreed.

"And it was coven night, and my friends all loved me, so they jumped right in."

"I work for a liquor distributor," Josh chimed in. "We don't drink a lot, but when we do, there's a supply."

Macklin had to chuckle. "I wish I'd known you when *I* was fresh out of college," he said, and the rest of the table laughed weakly.

"Anyway," Jordan resumed, a small smile on that handsome face in addition to the high color, "so we were a little boozy, and we all had… well, things we wanted out of life that we weren't getting. So I proposed a heart's desire spell. We have notes—you can see the candle we lit, the threads that bound it, even the words we used to execute the spell. But I don't think any of that is what matters."

Mack cocked his head. This was true, and it was something that most hedge witches took years to understand. The colors, the flowers, the oils, the metals—they were all important in that they had a history and the weight of human expectation in the elements' properties of communing with the natural, magical world. But the human intention and the direction in which it was aimed, that was key.

"What happened?" he asked, his curiosity incredibly aroused.

"Well, we all had our own personal heart's desire words written down, and we were supposed to say the spell together, and then each recite our own little poem, asking for the thing we wanted most."

Mack frowned. "That's solid spellcasting. What went wrong?"

Jordan's face went thunderous with self-recrimination, but to Macklin's surprise—and apparently everybody else's at the table as well—Bartholomew was the one who spoke up.

"We lied," he said softly. "Our little poems…. They were all lies. My little poem said something about my bakery business thriving, but that's not what I really wanted. So we were all ready to read those lies, one after another, but after the first incantation, the cone of power rose, and it was… well, it's gotten that big since,

but this was the first time we'd seen it so big and so…
so *bright*!"

Alex took up the thread. "It was the most power
we'd ever seen. You could make out everybody's
particular color. I'm probably the weakest witch here,
and that was one bright and shiny emerald green."

"And then," Kate said, "as this huge cone raised
itself above our heads, the magic *ripped* the words out
of us. Or I should say, *one word*. Everybody's heart's
desire, boiled down to one concrete word."

"And then we were knocked on our asses,"
Josh finished with a grimace. "Which is sort of what
happened when we cast the spell on the table. Fuckin'
magic, knockin' us on our ass."

Macklin winced. "Ouch," he said. He'd been there.

"Sayin'," Josh agreed.

"So seven of you cast a spell, and the spell
backfired—"

Jordan shook his head. "It's more personal than
that," he said. "The magic itself was offended. We
hadn't just told a polite lie on paper—we'd told a polite
lie to *ourselves*."

Mack nodded. "That's harder. That calls for a
personal reckoning." He looked around the earnest
faces at the table. "Have we all had that?"

"Yes. And those of us here have confessed to the
people we've needed to."

"Give me an example." Macklin was… intrigued?
All these people seemed so, well, *honest*.

And those honest people all glanced at each
other sideways, embarrassed to their bones.
Unsurprisingly, Josh of the copious muscles was the
one who spoke up.

"Like, Kate and I were getting super stressed about getting married. We wanted to be together forever, right, but all the other stuff was killing us. So I was thinking she was going to say 'breakup,' and she thought I was going to say 'elopement,' and I'd written, 'Please God, let her mother get off her back about losing weight for the dress,' or something like that and…." He frowned. "What'd you write, babe?"

She laughed a little. "Something about let us find a venue that my parents don't have to pay for. The rhyme was atrocious, but then—" She shrugged, her brown hair waving around her shoulders as she did. "—my heart wasn't in it."

"So," Macklin asked, pulled in. "What was your one word?"

They both grinned at each other, their eyes crinkling in the corners. "Baby!" Kate giggled, and her boyfriend gave a sort of endearing nose wrinkle in agreement.

"All we wanted was to be together and start our family," Josh agreed. "So that was easy." He winked at Kate and looked up at Macklin, his joy with his mate easing as he included the rest of the room into their bubble. "It *was* easy, because we were already together, and being honest wasn't going to change that. It…." He swallowed, and the others shared a glance with him. "It wasn't so easy for everybody else. Particularly…." He bit his lip.

"I'll tell that part," Jordan said softly.

Josh nodded, troubled, and Macklin's attention was once again fixed on the increasingly intense Jordan Bryne. Deliberately, Mack took the breadbasket and pulled out a slice to butter.

"So," he said, "was that the kind of secret everybody else was keeping?"

"Miscommunication?" Jordan said, shaking his head. "No."

Macklin's gaze darted to Alex and Bartholomew, who were sharing sheepish expressions with each other.

"I had a crush on my boss," Alex said. "I asked for the calf strength to ride my bike to another branch of my business so I could escape him."

Macklin sputtered in the act of raising the bread to his lips. "That's... that's...."

"Incredibly stupid," Alex said dryly. "I know. The word that got ripped out of my mouth was 'passion,' 'cause I'm just not that guy."

"That you knew of," Bartholomew whispered.

Alex grinned, very pleased with himself. "That I knew of," he said. His ginger complexion went crimson. "Turns out my boss was crushing too, and now he's my boyfriend." Alex sobered, his complexion leveling out. "It was his idea to go for help," he added. "We were killing ourselves trying to contain this disaster. Please don't be a douche."

Macklin took a bite of the bread and chewed on autopilot, suitably chastened.

And then the taste and texture of the bread sank in—solid, chewy, fortifying, and as he swallowed, a sense of strength and well-being spread throughout his body.

It was like drinking an elaborately brewed elixir of strength, and as the feeling suffused him, he turned wondering eyes to Jordan, who gave a very unsubtle glance to the shy little baker.

"Oh my Goddess," Macklin said. Bartholomew's eyes grew extraordinarily large, and Macklin thought he was going to run away, but Jordan's kind hand on his arm stopped him.

"He's impressed, Barty," Jordan said quietly. "We've been telling you. It's a real gift."

"Thanks, Jordan," Bartholomew said.

Macklin took a breath and shuddered. "That's *amazing*," he breathed. "That sustained me right to my bones. Are you our wizard?"

Bartholomew shook his head. "No. I just bake." A tiny smile flashed at the corners of his mouth, and a sympathetic smile tugged at Macklin's lips in turn.

"There's no 'just' about it," he said. "Thank you for sharing your bread with me."

The wariness that had clouded Bartholomew's eyes since Macklin's first clumsy entrance faded, and Macklin breathed a sigh of relief.

These were such nice people, he realized, and he found he wanted them to trust him.

"Okay," Macklin said, getting a clearer picture. "So you all told the polite lie, and nobody's wish was truly selfish—"

"Mine was," Jordan and Bartholomew said at the same time.

"Yours was not," Jordan chided.

"I wanted Lachlan," Bartholomew answered, his voice ringing clearer as he seemed to gain his courage. "That's why I put something about my business instead. You're not supposed to make other people love you."

Macklin let out a whistle. "So how was that resolved?" he asked, more out of curiosity than need to know.

Alex let out a snort. "They were both so gone on each other by the time we did the spell, all they needed was a nudge."

Josh let out a guffaw. "Yeah. That's what you call a love spell accidentally cast on two hundred people. A nudge!"

Macklin had arrived full of urgency and ire, but now, munching on Bartholomew's magic baking and listening to the give and take between this little coven, he realized that he really had nowhere else to be.

"Tell me the story," he asked, and by the time the group was done relating Bartholomew's epic sprint through a packed sci-fi convention, followed by adoring legions who loved him for his baking, he was a little tired, a little sated, and oddly comfortable with this group of people.

He didn't do comfortable a lot. Growing up the third son of the third son of a long line of wizards made for rigorous training in your childhood and a lot of rebellion in your adolescence.

And not many friends you could talk to about things like movies and traveling and your heart's desire.

It was too bad he was supposed to show up and fix this problem and then bail, but if he stayed, well, there were complications.

The laughter died down a little, and Macklin looked at the ever-intense Jordan. "I'd ask about your one word, but I have a feeling you've been naked enough tonight. It's almost three a.m. Are you going to tell me about the elephants not in the room?"

Jordan sucked in a breath and then leaned over the table, hands folded in front of him, and Macklin found himself swallowing convulsively, lured in by the intensity of those eyes. "Dante Vianelli and Cully Cromwell are the remaining two members of our coven. They room together in the stucco house in the middle, and Josh and Kate are on the end. Dante's a freelance journalist , keeps trying to find his craftiness, and we used to think he was our second most powerful witch until we realized what Bartholomew was really capable of. He's a big Italian guy with a blunt sense of humor and a laugh that could light up the room. His roommate, Cully, is a tiny little twink who is to sewing as Bartholomew is to baking—a creative and magical genius. But Cully isn't as focused as Barty, and he's a little high-maintenance. The only one—and I mean *only person*—on the planet who can maintain Cully, and their dog Glinda here, is Dante. They were not lovers. Ever. And that's really important in what I'm about to tell you."

Macklin's own eyes grew wide. "Uhm—"

"Who's got the picture?" Jordan asked, and Alex popped up.

"I do. I'll go fetch it."

Jordan nodded, a shock of blond hair falling forward, making him seem… touchable. "The morning after we cast the spell, all seven of us loaded up the van for Barty's convention, and then Dante and Cully walked home. Alex remembers seeing them walking away. They were holding hands. Which they didn't do. But they were standing like longtime lovers, and we think that's important too."

"Did they disappear? Take off? Fall through a portal, like I did?"

Jordan shook his head. "Worse. They went home, and then they started phasing through space and time like ghosts in a whirlpool. We've gone into their house several times. Even brought Lachlan and Simon, who didn't know them before this started. And for a while, they couldn't hear each other or see each other. But they could hear and see us, talk to us even, like they were just living their lives. They get groceries delivered. I've taken their trash to the curb, and the bins are getting full—like real people, mind you. But inside that house, they're walking through walls and calling each other's names. Cully's sewing machine is going at all hours of the night, and he keeps throwing dresses and costumes through—*through*—his wall to land on the couch, which is some freaky shit, trust me. Dante's computer is going. My dad owns this property. We rent from him. I checked to make sure Dante and Cully paid their rent on the first of October, and sure enough, they did."

Macklin took a deep breath. "Oh dear Goddess. What in the…? Have they been like this since *September*?"

"The autumn equinox," Jordan confirmed, those lean lips quirking. "And yes, I know Samhain is in ten or so days. Not stupid."

"Can you talk to them?" This sounded bad—so bad.

"We do, but they're… they're not really there. They *sound* like Dante and Cully, but like the cartoon versions. Not… not like their soul is really there. It's like the real person is trapped in the persona."

Macklin frowned. He'd probably have to see that for himself. "Do they know time is passing?" Because that was a hell of a long time to be trapped in a spell.

"I don't think so," Kate said. "We started putting *X*'s on the calendar, and our initials by them, so they could have… I don't know. *Proof* that time was passing, because they don't seem to see it."

"If nothing else," Alex said, "they should be interested in the *dog*. They're nuts about the damned dog, and they seem to think we're just taking her for a walk or a day or something. It's—" He swallowed. "—disquieting."

"Has there been *any* change?" Macklin asked.

They all nodded, and Jordan flattened one of his hands and waved it over the surface of the table. "This. We were trying to come up with a spell to sync them in time. Alex did all the groundwork for this one: a black candle in the center, colored candles in twelve shades all around, and an element for intention at every candle, colors matching."

"Both mutable and immutable," Alex said. "So cinnamon and lavender and licorice with garnet and amethyst and onyx."

"Did you all recite the spell?" Macklin asked, unnerved. There were five of them there—five witches and twelve quadrants of the clock—which made for very wonky magic.

"No," Alex said. "Jordan, Barty, and me."

A much better number. Goddess, for hedge witches, these people were smart—and damned good.

"What happened?" Macklin was starting to notice small things. Kate kept nodding off. Alex was hiding yawns behind his hand. Jordan had dark circles under his eyes. It was occurring to him that these people had been under an enormous amount of strain for a good long time.

"The cone of power came up," Kate said.

"All the lights went out," Josh continued.

"The magic charged," Alex added.

"And then it blew up," Bartholomew huffed.

"Leaving this on the table," Jordan finished. "And knocking us on our asses."

"And sending the dog to Simon's," Alex said glumly. "Damn, I'm glad that stopped happening."

"Your dog disappeared?" Macklin gasped. It was like a horror movie in these nice people's living room. Except it was real.

"*Dante and Cully's* dog disappeared," Alex said sourly. "We've been taking care of her since…." He waved his hands. "It was the second time it happened. She ended up at my boss's house, and that led to me and Simon getting together, and Simon goes, 'Hey, I'm only a manager of my own firm, but if I were you guys, I'd look for some help, right?'"

"And you called me." And now Macklin *really* felt like a heel about how he'd strode in here, assuming a bunch of backward hedge witches had fucked with him for kicks. No wonder Jordan had been so aggressive. He was starting to get it now. "Was that everything that happened?"

"No," Jordan said. He took the picture from Alex and showed him.

Macklin saw two people—one tall with dark hair and a valiant nose and chin and the other delicate and perky, with blond hair and slightly unfocused blue eyes. They were at the beach, wearing sweaters stretched out and loved by time, and leaning together like lovers did when they'd been together for a while and would continue to be together for a long time afterward.

Macklin frowned. "But you said they weren't lovers."

Everybody nodded.

Jordan said, "And that's where things get really weird."

AN hour later, Macklin had to call it quits. They'd explained to him about the shifting memories and the way everybody in the coven could imagine a Dante and Cully who *were* together versus a Dante and Cully who *weren't*. He'd extracted every detail of every spell from all involved and looked at the meticulous notes kept by Jordan and Alex.

By the time he was done, Josh and Kate had crashed on the couch, leaning against each other, the dog across their laps, and Bartholomew had cleaned up the table before sitting down and falling asleep where he sat. Alex remained awake—barely—by propping his chin on his hands.

Jordan appeared to be keeping his ice-blue eyes open by sheer will and vengeance, though, answering Macklin's questions promptly and without artifice.

And Macklin got why the table was important, because they'd managed to cut through three days' worth of distrust and getting-to-know-you by sitting down and telling him every damned thing they could.

But it had taken them over three weeks to dig themselves this deep—he wasn't going to be able to help them muddle through that night.

He shoved back from the table with a yawn and offered a conciliatory smile at Jordan. "So," he said. "Whose couch am I sleeping on?"

Alex yawned. "Kate and Josh have a spare bedroom. You sleep there. Barty'll sleep on Jordan's couch. Boom."

"Doesn't Bartholomew live here?" Macklin asked, squinting his eyes.

"The witch's house is a whole new experience," Jordan said behind a yawn. "And I've got to get there if we're getting up at seven to perform the ritual."

Macklin glanced around, surprised. "You perform a sunrise ritual *every* morning?"

"We do if we don't want the neighborhood to go to hell," Jordan said on another yawn. "Here—let me wake Josh and Kate."

Jordan moved to the couch, and Macklin looked over at Alex. "How bad is the witch's cottage?" he asked quietly.

Alex's eyes went wide, and he shuddered. "Bad."

"I'll sleep on the couch there," Macklin said, thinking to make up for being a complete asshole.

Alex's mouth twisted in clear skepticism. "Sure. You do that."

"I was trying to be nice!" Macklin objected, but Alex jerked away from the table—and not in time.

"Ouch!" he hissed. "Remember where we are!"

"Wait," Mack muttered. "I don't understand. What lie did I tell?"

"You couldn't care less about being nice," Alex told him irritably. "You've got the same glint in your eyes everybody gets when they want to sleep with Jordan. Jesus, can you keep it in your pants for a minute? Can't you see he's worried sick?"

Macklin's mouth dropped slowly open, and he barely remembered himself enough to tell Jordan about the change of plans.

Dammit. *Dammit.* Alex, the accountant and self-proclaimed weakest witch of the coven, had just told Macklin something he hadn't even acknowledged in his own head.

Exhausted, on edge, kind and supportive or glaring and intense, Jordan Bryne seemed to be hitting all Macklin's sweet spots, but Jordan was in no position at all to reciprocate Macklin's slow-burning desire.

The House of the Rising Sun

JORDAN accepted Macklin's offer to sleep on the couch, but only because he knew Bartholomew and Alex were exhausted and on their last nerve.

He led the way across the lawn, taking care to avoid the sleeping bodies of the squirrels, who always dropped off where they'd been marching without so much as an eyelash flutter. He stepped over the limp little forms and made sure a couple of bowls of water and some shelled nuts, which had been set out at strategic points in their infinity-symbol formation, were full. He also eyeballed the birdseed in feeder bowls under the eaves of the middle house, where a murder of crows slumbered on the rain gutters, making sure they were doing okay too.

It didn't seem fair that the animals co-opted to make their lives miserable had to starve or run until they dropped. This wasn't their fight, right?

And speaking of fight, two of the cats were on the lawn, sitting on their haunches, paws columned in front of them, ears perked like sentinels. One was enormous, fluffy, and gray, and the other was a tiny, light-boned calico. Both of them swiveled their heads unnervingly and gave Macklin the once-over as he approached.

The gray one inclined his head regally, but the calico sniffed and started washing her paw.

"Hey, guys," Jordan said softly. He held out a piece of the salami Bartholomew had put on the meat-and-cheese plate and let the gray one take it from his fingers. The calico gave him a disdainful look, and he laid another piece down a respectful distance from her.

Her glance this time was a little more benign, and she ate the delicacy with a dainty little bite.

"Keep up the good work, guys," Jordan told them, wishing he had names for them. "I appreciate all you do."

The calico went back to washing her paw, but the gray one gave a composed nod of the head. Well, that was nice. Jordan had bought nine bowls and nine cat beds, which he placed on the back porch, with one of those "replenishing" water bowls as well. He wasn't sure what Helen had fed the cats when she'd lived there, but he got the sense they were dedicated guardians of the cottage. Even before the spell backfired, he and the others had been invested in keeping them healthy and well cared for.

"You like cats?" Macklin asked as they made their way up the walk.

"I didn't really think about them," Jordan admitted. "And then Helen gave me the keys to this place and took off on her Ducati, and the cats and I sort of had to adjust to each other." He smiled fondly; when the gray one went off shift, he usually came to sleep next to Jordan in the full-sized bed. "The gray one is sort of my personal guardian. We get on very well, and someday I should like to name him."

The cat closed his eyes halfway in a sort of benevolent "isn't he cute" gesture, and Jordan waved good night.

"They come and go through a pet door in the back. Some of them are strictly outside cats, but some of them like a good scratch around the ears when it suits them."

Macklin made a sleepy sound of surprise. "That's a lot of effort for animals you inherited when a crazy old woman gave you her keys."

Jordan shrugged. "Yeah, well, I think everybody else would have helped me by adopting one or two and spreading the work out, but they sort of belong to the house."

He put his hand on the doorknob then and went to unlock it, but something…. The heat of the knob, maybe, or perhaps it was the smell.

"Fuck! Stand back!" He threw the door open and sent out a blanket spell, quelling the twelve black candles that had assembled themselves in the center of the tiny living room and lit themselves while they were at it.

The flames quenched immediately in response to his will, and Jordan glared at the spot still burning in the center of the carpet. The ember went out, leaving a small trail of acrid smoke drifting toward the ceiling.

He took a hint and looked up, not surprised by the nine-sided star inscribed there in the black smoke from the black candles.

"Thanks," he told the ceiling. "I get it. There's nine of us now if Dante and Cully come back. You need a full complement of witches. Whatever. If you burn the place down before we get there, you're shit out of luck, so stop trying that, okay?"

With that he hit the light switch on the wall and three lamps came on, shedding a graceful yellow light on the living room.

Much of the room was taken up by a library of spell-crafting books—a gift well respected and well loved by Jordan's coven. The books seemed to like his people too. Jordan knew that when somebody took a book home and spent the night looking for a spell, they might wake up in the morning and find the book opened to exactly what they needed but hadn't found.

Two tiered glass cases, each with three shelves, took up one end of the room. One was filled with crystal decanters, all of them labeled with a specific oil distillation, and the other held various stones, most of them in small groupings inside velveteen bags. A few of the stones, though—the ones Jordan and the coven used the most—were the size of paperweights, polished and smooth, and sat openly on the shelves.

There were additional shelves everywhere—on the walls, in the corners—filled with everything from packets of drying herbs to tarot decks. Jordan had counted seventeen different decks when he'd moved in but had bought his own because he didn't want to take anything away from Helen—like control over her own cards—that she wasn't willing to give.

But Jordan ignored all of these things now, including the smell of burned candlewicks, sage, and vetiver, and instead moved to the couch, where a small pile of bedding and a pillow sat. He nodded to the pile and said, "Make yourself at home. I've got pajama pants if you want them. The heater refuses to click on unless the temperature drops below sixty in here, so you may want them."

Macklin grimaced. "That's nice of you," he muttered. "God, I don't even have any clothes. Or a toothbrush. And I *smell*."

Jordan chuckled softly. "Our apologies?" he offered. "Anyway, you're actually closer to Dante's size than anyone's. Or… wait! Lachlan is coming tomorrow. I'll have him bring you some spare clothes." He gestured into the bedroom, which had housed a bed and not much else when he'd moved in. He'd brought in a couple of dressers for his clothes, since apparently there was no such thing as *closets* where Helen came from, and he and Dante had spent a day installing cupboards on one wall so he could house towels and linens and shampoo and things. He pulled out a clean toothbrush from a pack of them, handed it over, and nodded to the bathroom, which was only accessible from the bedroom.

"I'm sorry. It lacks privacy of any form, but I promise no orgies have happened in here, ever, and I don't sleep naked."

"Shame," Macklin said dryly, running sleepy eyes up and down Jordan's admittedly long body.

Jordan caught his breath, the pull—the magnetic, maddening pull he'd felt to Macklin since the man strode into their lives—hitting him hard in the belly.

He sent Macklin a fulminating glance and shook his head.

"We can't," he said. "Not even flirting. Don't you understand? There are too many important things to do in the next ten days. My friends have been trapped for nearly a *month*, and I am *terrified* for them!"

Macklin held out his hands in that universally placating gesture that usually pissed more people off than it calmed down. "Sorry! Sorry! I was just… I don't know… making a joke?"

Jordan blew out a breath and knuckled his forehead, right where that stubborn muscle kept clenching between his eyes. "I'm sorry too," he muttered. "Look, I know it's been an unusual night for you, but it's been sort of a month for me and my friends. I would really, really like to get a few hours of sleep before sunrise, okay?"

"I hear you," Macklin agreed. "I'll shower in the morning."

"I'll set out some sweats for you," Jordan told him. "After the ritual I'll probably come back and sleep for a couple of hours—lucky us, we all took time off work for the next few weeks to deal with whatever is coming, but it's not gonna be a vacation. After the nap, I'll need to spend the day clearing out the garden. The others can answer your questions if you need them. I, uh, I find that if I don't keep up with things like the garden, bad things happen."

"Like candles spontaneously combusting in your living room?" Macklin prompted.

"Well, last fall I put off cleaning out the garden and got rotten tomatoes flinging themselves at the entire side of the house. I need to get it done by Samhain or I'm fucked."

Macklin shook his head. "Man, I was *raised* for this level of maintenance. I was riding my motorcycle through Nevada to get away from the clutter of witchcraft and magic left over from a shitty childhood, and you just took that woman's keys and ran with it?"

Jordan blinked slowly. "You were raised with magic?" he asked, his voice a little breathy with awe. "That's wonderful. To know that it's real? To be born knowing you could control it?" He glanced around the witch's cottage. "I think something like this? This took her a lifetime to build, stacking spell upon spell, ritual upon ritual, until every nook and cranny has a life and a story of its own. Now, I'd rather those stories and nooks and crannies were *my* own, but that doesn't mean I don't respect them. I think that's why Helen gave the place to me—she knew I'd keep it for her until she returned. And I have. And now I want to build a place just for me."

Macklin nodded, giving the tiny cottage a once-over. "Make yours bigger," he said thoughtfully. "With more natural light."

A chuckle—a real one—welled up from Jordan's stomach. "My father's a contractor. I was raised in a house that looks like it should be in movies. All the space you could ask for and a breakfast nook. Don't worry, when I find my own place, I'll make sure I don't have to duck under the doorframes."

Macklin rubbed his forehead in sympathy—apparently he'd noticed Jordan lowering his head by sheer instinct. "Bruises?"

Jordan nodded. "And a concussion after I first moved in. So, so not helpful."

Macklin smiled, and for a quiet, sleepy moment, they were two men standing in close proximity in Jordan's bedroom. Jordan closed his eyes and smelled creosote bush and leather and sweat. He must have rocked a little on his feet because when he opened his eyes, Macklin's chiseled features were so much closer, those dark blue eyes surrounded by thick black lashes, the pupils so wide in the center they almost filled out the entire iris.

Macklin leaned in and kissed Jordan's cheek, and the action sent Jordan backing up hurriedly.

"What was that for?" he gasped.

"Tiredness," Macklin said promptly. "Spite. Attraction. Take your pick. I'm going to go lie on the couch and try to keep your place from burning itself down." He smiled and sauntered toward the door, only to stop when the lights in the cottage flickered off, then flickered on purple, then flickered off, then flickered on green, and then flickered off again.

He sucked in a breath. "Does it do that all night?" he asked.

"No. But pretty soon we're going to get one of the greatest hits of the 1960s played from two blocks away through the walls. No, I don't know which song will be on repeat tonight. Whichever one it will be, you will not stop humming it all day tomorrow. I apologize in advance."

Macklin groaned right when the opening guitar riff of "House of the Rising Sun" drifted in through the walls.

"Are you kidding me?" he asked from the doorway. True to form, the music was barely quiet enough to make it possible to fall asleep while listening to it, but loud enough to seep into the dreams of anyone in the cottage.

"Could be worse," Jordan said. "I had a week of 'Wichita Lineman' last winter. Enjoy."

As Jordan shut the door, he heard Macklin—in a rather sweet baritone—singing about being a lineman for the county in direct counterpoint to "House of the Rising Sun."

He was—contrary to all things—chuckling as the door clicked shut.

A SCANT few hours later, the windup clock on his dresser went off ten minutes before sunrise. Jordan grabbed three tea-sized candles from the big box in the cupboard—yellow for wisdom, blue for creativity, and white for new beginnings and protection. He texted Barty to bring him some black thread to banish negative influences and then threw on a hoodie over his tee and pajama pants, slid on his flip-flops, and headed out the door.

He passed Macklin, who was huddled deep under the blanket and comforter he'd left on the couch, sleeping like he needed it. With his eyes closed and his face relaxed in sleep, Macklin appeared softer, like people did. Jordan could see beyond the piercing blue of his gaze and on to the soft lips, which seemed like they had a tendency to smile, and the laugh lines at the corners of his eyes and mouth.

He may have stalked into Barty's house pissed and ready for bear, but he apparently wasn't like that all the time.

Good to know. They were going to have to work with him.

Jordan ignored the tightening in his belly, the way his jaw and forehead softened when he watched Macklin sleep, the way his mouth went a little dry. He'd meant what he'd said just hours before—he didn't have *time* for that.

Besides, wasn't Jordan's lovelorn bullshit what had gotten them all into this jam in the first place?

The dark morning was cold, and his breath fogged into the dismal, grayish light. He used to love this time of day, right before sunrise, but this last month, trying to beat the sun so they could harness its strength to keep their neighborhood from falling apart, had changed dawn from an exciting time to face the possibilities of a new day into a desperate race to keep away the darkness.

Still, as he made his way across the frosty grass to the middle of the street, he rubbed the smooth wax of the candles and had some hope.

He got out to the pretaped stars they'd inscribed in the center of the cul-de-sac and set the candles in the middle, smiling when Alex and Bartholomew greeted him with the thread he'd asked for. He was binding the candles together when a pair of pink bunny slippers and another pair of stuffed Tasmanian Devil slippers slid into his view.

Josh and Kate had arrived.

"Trying something new?" Alex asked as Jordan straightened.

"Maybe some solid elements will give the spell some permanence?" Jordan guessed. "It's been fraying at the edges every evening, and when we got to the cottage last night, it was about to set itself on fire again."

They all cast fulminating glares at the witch's cottage, and Jordan had to admit it had become a sort of daunting taskmaster over the past year and a half. When he'd first taken over stewardship from Helen, they'd been able to leave for a couple of days. Jordan would visit his dads and stay overnight, or they'd all go on the weekend trips that they'd so enjoyed during college. But gradually the amount of time Jordan had been able to be gone without the cottage threatening codependent bullshit on him, like throwing kitty roca over the fences into the neighbors' yards or, hey, *setting itself on fire*, had become shorter and shorter. Now, apparently, he could be gone for sixteen hours max.

As though reading his thoughts, Bartholomew said, "That would be a bad thing? Right? We're thinking that would be a bad thing?"

Jordan glanced over his shoulder and grimaced. "I've gotten fond of the cats," he said. "And the library has been quite helpful."

They all nodded. "The library seems to like us," Kate said. "Do you think it would follow?"

They were all quiet for long enough that Jordan had to shake himself to remember the sun was about to rise.

"Right. Everybody."

They all held hands, and Jordan looked at the sunrise, the gold, the orange, and the deep blue of it, and with a quick, hard glance at the candles, lit their wicks with merely a thought. As the flames bloomed, he performed the recitation.

We have faith in the new day,
Have learned from the old
Have the strength of heart our promises to hold.

"After me," he instructed.

Then he broke it down, one piece at a time, and the group recited after him as the glow of their power coalesced in the center of their inscribed star, above the candles.

He finished off with "May we be in step with time and space once more. So may it be."

"So may it be," everybody finished after him, and they all watched as the cone of power they'd raised burst, spreading sparkles of magic throughout the cul-de-sac and, hopefully, the neighborhood beyond, lifting the pall that fell over the light, the land, *everything* within their gaze's reach between rituals.

They all took a breath that was freer now than it had been when Jordan had ventured out into the cold, and Jordan rubbed his hands together to warm them.

"Back to sleep for a few hours?" he asked the group, and they all nodded, hiding yawns behind their hands.

"Breakfast, our house, elevenish," Bartholomew said, yawning. "Got a call this morning to say my craft fair got canceled—I guess the venue sprung a leak. So you guys get to be my guinea pigs for apple crumble bars."

Kate turned adoring eyes on him. "You are my favorite," she said sincerely. "We have some vegan sausage, and a happy client gave Josh two dozen fresh eggs. We'll be there with presents." She smiled hopefully at Jordan.

Jordan smiled back. "I have a basket of red and green peppers and tomatoes," he confirmed. "And I bought a bag of mushrooms for the occasion."

"In another four hours, that's gonna sound *banging*," Josh told them, the words muffled behind his hand as he yawned. "See you all then." He held out his fist for the bump, which was not exactly witchy but *was* very much a part of who they'd been from long before Helen had given Jordan the keys to her cottage.

They did a massive fist bump and flameout, happy in a way Jordan hadn't seen them in a while. He had to wonder as he made his way back up the driveway to the cottage if that was a result of the new candles or the successful call for help.

As he opened the door to the cottage, he gazed out over the neighborhood and saw the squirrels starting their infinity march, the turkeys judging Kate and Josh's house, and three giant barn owls—a new addition— swooping in to nap, one apiece, on everybody's chimneys. He studied the road that led into the cul-de-sac, across from which sat a vacant field, and saw that the snakes that usually populated the apple trees were all snake-sneaking back through the field, and the nine cats of the clowder had roused themselves from their nightly activities and were taking up formation on the front lawn.

Grimly, he decided it didn't matter. If he could give his troops any hope at all to combat despair in their battle, he was going to grab that with both hands.

He let himself in, closed the door behind him, and tried to tiptoe past the figure burrowed in the blankets on the couch. He'd seen Macklin's motorcycle parked on the street between the cottage and Alex and Barty's, with the helmet dangling from the handlebars. It had been a big, battered black beast of a machine—not showy, no sidesaddles or extensions. Nothing but a powerful motor and a sturdy frame.

Jordan had coveted it quietly, even though his dads would have had a heart attack if he so much as thought of taking one of those things for a spin.

Macklin apparently heard his thoughts—or his quiet footsteps—because he yawned and sat up, the covers slipping down an impressive bare chest dusted with black hair.

"Are you really up?" he said through his yawn.

"No, just the sunrise ritual. Go back to sleep. We're gathering at Barty and Alex's for brunch at eleven."

Macklin frowned. "I was going to watch your ritual," he mumbled. "I set my phone."

Jordan grimaced. "Yeah, sorry about that. Phones haven't worked since the big spell. I mean, texting, phoning, internet, yes. Setting alarms and keeping time? Not so much. And they suck power through a straw, so you're going to need to charge it soon. I've got a windup clock in my room—the only reason I've kept my job."

Macklin yawned again and swung his legs out over the bed. Legs, Jordan noted, that were muscular, tanned, and lightly covered with the same dark hair that was on his chest. Ugh—did everything about the man *have* to be so appealing?

"I'm gonna go pee before you go back to sleep. That's probably the only reason I woke up, since apparently phones don't work."

"Knock yourself out," Jordan said. "Timer on the coffeepot still works. Let me set it up for ten thirty while you go."

Jordan did that, and Macklin disappeared through his bedroom. When he came back, he had a towel over his shoulders, probably to keep him from freezing in the house.

"There you go," Jordan said with a final twist of the manual clock. "My dads were using it from a zillion years ago. I asked if I could borrow it since phones aren't working."

"Did they ask why?" Macklin said, sliding back into his happy little burrow.

Jordan glanced at him, surprised. "Oh, I don't keep anything from the dads. They've known about the witchcraft since the get-go. Sebastian asks me to come over and cleanse their house every time my dad has a company dinner. Apparently there's a spouse or two Sebastian doesn't care for, and he likes to shoo away their bad vibes, as he calls them."

Macklin chuckled. "The exit of the suburban bitch is the bread and butter of a good hedge witch," he said.

"Or bastard," Jordan added, frowning.

"Yeah. My family is sort of a sexist throwback— and bastard doesn't rhyme."

Jordan snorted, glad he acknowledged it. "Is that a quote?" he asked.

"Sort of a maxim in my family." Macklin turned on his side and watched as Jordan switched the light off in the kitchen and cut across the living room. "Mm…," he mumbled. "Whatever you did outside, you smell like sunshine and cedar, burnt leaves, coffee, and something blue. Good smells. Sweet dreams, hedge witch. I'm gonna dream about your smells and the rising sun."

Jordan paused as he passed the couch. "You are going to regret being quite so adorable when you wake up," he told Macklin. "I'll forget you said that."

Macklin regarded him steadily with those dark-fringed eyes. "Don't," he said. "Maybe this is a side of me that doesn't come out to play that often."

Jordan's mouth quirked. "I get the feeling parts of you have gotten quite a lot of play." He waited until Macklin's eyes widened in outrage—and appreciation—of the pun before he turned and walked away. "I'll wake you at ten thirty," he called.

"Deal!"

Build Me Up, Buttercup

MACKLIN paused in the walk from Jordan's house to Alex and Bartholomew's and, stepping gingerly to avoid the familiars yawning and stretching on the lawn of the house, went to study the altar in the center of the cul-de-sac.

It was mostly a taped—and retaped and drawn and redrawn—series of stars, starting with a three-pointed star closer to the center of the cul-de-sac, a five-pointed star a little farther out, and a seven-pointed star a few feet farther out from that. He wondered who stood in for the seven-pointed star, remembered there were boyfriends who pitched in when they were there, and spent his time concentrating on the feel of the magic rising up from each star instead.

Oh! They were all so strong!

At the three-pointed star, he could smell Jordan's cedar and sunshine smell, Bartholomew's sugar and vanilla, and vague hints of the smell of wind—which was probably Alex, who had a runner's or cyclist's body. Flowers—Kate. And meatloaf.

Meatloaf?

Macklin moved to the five-pointed star, where those very definite smells were present, as well as the scent of pine dust and lemon oil and... was that teakwood cologne?

The boyfriends.

He smiled a little to himself, then looked up to Jordan Bryne's patient regard.

"Sorry," he said, brow furrowing. "I was just getting a feel for everybody's magic."

Jordan nodded. "Figured," he said. "Come on. You can talk to everybody some more." He indicated a small black Prius with a nod of his head. "That's Alex's boyfriend, and he probably brought Bartholomew's with him."

"Pine and lemon, and men's cologne?"

Jordan blinked and smiled a little. "Yes. I tend to see it as colors—Lachlan is pine-and-lemon smelling, but I see him as the color of the table he made. Simon smells like men's cologne, but I see him as black—not because he's pure magic but because he's pure reason. His one true talent seems to be the absence of magic and an appreciation of it. What does everyone else smell like?"

Macklin took a few more steps toward the squirrels, and now that they were moving on their sort of endless march of doom, he felt sorry for them. No wonder the coven left them shelled nuts and water; it seemed like such a dismal little existence.

"Well, Kate smelled floral—carnation and rose and a wee bit of amber—and Bartholomew smells like—"

"Let me guess. Cookies."

Macklin nodded and took a little leap to the center of the infinity symbol, and then one to the other side. He frowned. "There is no magic in the center of that. You'd think there would be."

"Maybe there's enough magic fueling the poor squirrels," Jordan said, leading up the path.

"So Alex? Who's emerald green to me, by the way."

"He smells like wind," Macklin said.

"Bicyclist," Jordan told him, and Macklin wanted to pump his fist. Score!

"So," Macklin asked delicately. "Uhm, Josh?"

"Salt of the earth," Jordan said softly. "White. Not very powerful, but very pure."

Macklin laughed. "Smells like meatloaf!"

And Jordan was laughing too as he opened the door.

What greeted them was the same group of people plus two—and a very impressive two. Alex's boyfriend was tall and slender, dressed in blue jeans and a black turtleneck with what appeared to be a newly acquired silver pentagram worn at his throat. He had dark shoulder-length hair, intelligent brown eyes, and a wicked smile—and eyes only for Alex, who gave him shy looks from under his lashes that made Macklin a little fond himself.

Bartholomew's boyfriend was both a surprise and exactly like Macklin imagined him. He was almost as tall as Jordan, with the build of a young lumberjack and reddish hair, a booming laugh, and a strongly handsome face, Macklin wondered exactly how the sublimely quiet Bartholomew had attracted this man's attention. But then seeing the adoration on Lachlan's face told him that maybe it was the innate fineness in both of them that had done the attracting.

Nice people, he thought, not for the first time. He was dealing with nice people. His father was rather horrible about hedge witches; wizards didn't deal with such penny-ante displays of magic. Macklin hadn't been allowed to even talk to hedge witches or their children growing up. His magic—and his father had made much of him being rated one of the strongest of his generation—was often sort of magnetic to anybody dealing with the arcane. When he'd been in college, he'd made use of that attraction rather shamelessly. Every boy loved a willing bed partner. As he'd grown, however, he'd realized the inherent dishonesty in it.

People were coming on to him because they felt his magic, and he was putting out for them, using the magic as an unspoken enticement he had no intention of giving away.

Since he'd had that realization, he'd become pickier about his bed partners. They had to be either a) magically blind, or b) powerful enough that they didn't *need* Macklin for anything.

Yes, it seemed calculated—and he'd turned down some genuinely nice people because of his rule of thumb—but he didn't hurt any feelings, either, or inspire any jealousies or make himself a target of any kind.

It was something the old man would have approved of heartily, had he known, and that made Macklin hate himself a little, but he hadn't thought of a better way so far.

Unconsciously his eyes followed Jordan as he washed his hands and put on an apron and started washing and chopping the vegetables in the bag he'd brought.

Macklin realized that the people in the kitchen—
Bartholomew, Lachlan, Jordan, Kate, and Alex—were
all moving in a complex sort of dance, as though they'd
all occupied that space before. He'd seen it in Kate and
Bartholomew when they'd made up their late-night
snack, but it was even more impressive now.

But that wasn't *really* why he was watching.

Jordan's long, lean body was a little awkward
when he first started, but as he relaxed into what was
obviously a common chore, the tenseness around his
eyes, his mouth, his shoulders—all of it disappeared.
He made light conversation with his friends, even
Lachlan, whom Macklin understood was new to the
little circle, and Jordan's stunning ice-blue eyes seemed
to melt a little with warmth.

"They're something to watch, aren't they?"

Macklin glanced at Simon, who had moved next to
him after Josh had gone outside with the little bichon
frise on a leash.

"Yeah," Macklin said. "They do this often?"

"Well, usually Bartholomew has an event—he
bakes his heart out every weekend and sells to sci-fi
and anime conventions and the like. Jordan makes oils
for the booth, and Kate makes soaps. I gather Cully"—
his voice dropped—"made things like sachets and
facecloths and such. So they all help Bartholomew out
so he can go sell their items. It's like a little co-op."

Macklin frowned. He'd met some covens who
were close before, but this? This was almost like the
wizard's compound he'd grown up in.

Except it didn't impart the smell of wet iron or the
cold feeling of chains.

"That's interesting," he said, keeping his eyes on
Jordan. "Everybody has day jobs?"

"Oh yes." Simon nodded. "Alex is my employee."
He wrinkled his nose. "Which sounds really douchey. I
swear I signed all sorts of things to make sure Alex isn't
going to get abused or anything. My business partners
would kill me if he quit because we broke up. I think
they really do love him best."

Macklin grinned at him because he was charming,
and for a moment, he *almost* thought he saw magic in
Simon's aura.

Then he realized that what he saw was *charm*.
Charm that had been cultivated with so much effort it
had a haze of its own.

But he also saw a sort of pale amber shimmer
around him, and that indicated good intentions.

Huh. So he was one of those people who worked
extra hard to put people at ease. Given how intense
Alex could be, that probably came in handy.

His eyes returned to Jordan, who was listening to
Kate tell a story about work with a furrow between his
brows.

"What did Josh say?" he heard Jordan ask.

"He says my boss is a douchebag, and I should
quit," she said glumly. "But I *like* this job." She
scowled at the cream she was whisking, possibly into
butter. "I like doing PR and ads and stuff. It's fun! It's
interesting! It's just that I don't like doing it for this
particular giant law firm that defends deadbeat dads."

Macklin grimaced.

"Well, maybe you could do some work for Barty
and Lachlan," Jordan said. "We're starting to get
backlogged with stock—if we could only get Barty
a venue that wouldn't break his bank, he could quit
his day job and open up a store, fronting for *all* of us,
right?"

Kate nodded thoughtfully. "That's occurred to me," she admitted. "That we're close, all of us, to being able to… I don't know. Make the leap beyond all this. Past our start-up jobs"—she eyeballed Alex—"unless our start-up job is our dream job. But, you know, everybody. We're ready to level up somehow."

Jordan grunted. "You're not wrong." He sighed, and the dejected droop of his shoulders hurt Macklin somehow. "But first…."

"Yeah." Kate's head bowed, and the brightness of the entire kitchen—done in colors of green and orange and red and navy blue—seemed to dim. "We've got to fix this thing we're working on. It's just really hard to get unstuck."

"Breakfast helps," Bartholomew said softly. "Behind you, Katy."

She stepped sideways smoothly, and Bartholomew opened the oven to pull out something that smelled like apples from heaven and cinnamon nirvana.

"How long have you all been… I don't know. A team?" Macklin asked.

"Well, *they've* been a team since their freshman year at college," Simon said. "*I've* only known Alex for the last three years. We hired him right out of school, after his internship at another firm." As Macklin watched, Simon's cheeks pinkened, and so did the edges of his ears, which made this very suave man Macklin's age look younger—and incredibly sincere. "Alex and I have only been a thing for a couple of weeks. But there was… longing," he finished with dignity. "Lots and lots of longing."

Macklin swallowed. He wanted to say, "I don't know what that feels like," but that would be too naked.

He didn't know Simon that well. He didn't know *anybody* in this little coven that well.

He eyed Jordan, tall and masculine, eyes narrowed as he tended to his task at the same time he took the pulse of the people he cared for. Macklin swallowed.

"Sounds nice," he said, feeling incredibly inadequate.

Simon snorted. "It was awkward and stupid, and I made an ass of myself about six hundred times a day." His lips twisted with remembered sweetness. "But it wasn't boring. And it's only gotten better."

At that moment Josh burst through the door, Glinda panting at his feet, saving Macklin from having to say something real.

"It is fuckin' cold out there!" he said, blowing on his hands. "My nipples could etch granite, I shit you not."

Jordan looked over his shoulder. "Is it that cold in the neighborhood, or only in the cul-de-sac."

"Just the cul-de-sac," Josh said, his voice full of apology.

"Fuck me!" Jordan snapped.

Macklin flinched at first, because he sounded angry, and then Kate said, "Jordan! Oh honey! Here's a towel. Go to the bathroom and dress that!"

"Goddammit," Jordan muttered, and then he was rushing out of the kitchen and toward the hall, pushing past Macklin and Simon in his hurry.

Macklin was scrambling after him before it even registered that someone else there might be a healer too.

Nobody followed him, though, so maybe if somebody *was* a healer, they either had their hands up to their elbows in breakfast or were lost in time in the house next door.

"Barty, where's your Band-Aids!" Jordan shouted as he rummaged one-handedly through the cupboard over the sink.

Macklin had entered a standard suburban-house bathroom, but it had bright green-and-blue towels and floor mats, as well as blue tile above the tub. Macklin was starting to enjoy this space, which by its nature should have been homogenous but wasn't.

"Here," he said brusquely. "Sit down. I'll get it."

"I don't need help," Jordan muttered.

"No, of course not," Macklin told him dryly, muscling his way next to Jordan to get access to the first-aid supplies. Jordan's long body was flush with heat, and he smelled like fresh vegetables and butter—mm! With a huff, Jordan sat down on the commode while Macklin searched. He found the cupboard well stocked, including a box of sterile gloves and a large container of gauze and tape, along with Band-Aids and ointment. "Do you guys skewer yourself regularly?" he asked, pulling out what he needed.

"Alex spills his bike sometimes. Barty gets burns. I'm forever cutting myself at work and need another bandage. We all got in the habit of stocking up when I roomed here."

"Must have been tight," Macklin muttered, washing his hands. "Don't you all have jobs?"

"Well, yeah," Jordan said, "but we were all starting out. And we were coming out of the dorms. Like Kate said, a good beginning place." He tried to look under the towel and grimaced. "Besides, Alex and Barty were sharing the larger room, so they got the worst of it. They still have full-sized beds even though they have their own rooms." He huffed out a breath. "It would be great if we could get the whole Dante and Cully thing resolved so they could at least buy queen-sized. I'm sure Simon and Lachlan would enjoy that very much."

"No sleepovers?" Macklin asked, sliding the gloves on. "Here, give me your hand."

Jordan peeled the towel off and threw it in the hamper in the corner before letting Macklin take his hand and put it under the running tap. Jordan hissed a little, but that was all, and considering the size of the slice down the side of his finger, that was pretty stoic.

"We need everybody here in the mornings," Jordan reminded him. "Which sucks because they've both waited so long to fall in love, and now they're all paying for my fuckup and can't actually get on with their lives."

"I don't think that's how any of them see it," Macklin murmured. "Okay, if you were with anyone else, I'd say you need stitches, but you're here with me, and I think I can bind it myself. But wow—just wow. Maybe stay out of the kitchen until you can focus on things like hot stoves and knives, okay?" Carefully he dumped some antibiotic cleanser on the wound, unsurprised when Jordan's hand went leaden in his grip.

"A butterfly bandage and some gauze would be fine," Jordan said coldly. "And I don't care how they see it. I was their leader, and now two of us are lost and the rest of us are stuck. 'Hey gang, let's do a heart's desire spell. It'll be tits!' God, like some college frat boy with a beer bong."

"Did you really say that?" Macklin challenged. "Did you really say 'It'll be tits!' Because if you did, I'm going to leave you right now. You all deserve your fates. You for saying it, them for listening to it."

He used a delicate touch as he patted the wound dry with the gauze, and Jordan snorted and shook his head, obviously unwilling to be soothed.

"Stop wiggling," Macklin ordered. He made sure the wound was clean and then lined the edges of it together and closed his eyes.

Bind together ragged skin
Ease the pain and soothe the soul
Be eased without and within
Once again be whole.

He murmured the spell without thought—he'd been taught the small chants practically from the cradle. When he was done, he blew on it, like a parent might blow on a slight burn, and watched as the skin reknit before his eyes, with only the faintest glow as it came together.

"Whoa," Jordan whispered, shivering a little. "That's impressive."

Macklin, moved by the same impulse that had led him to kiss Jordan's cheek, folded that long-fingered hand with his gloved ones and raised it to his lips. He placed a final healing benediction on the faint scar of the recent cut.

And felt the tingle of wellness—and of connection—right down to his groin.

He actually heard Jordan swallow as he tried to reclaim his hand.

"Thank you," he said stiffly. "I should go—"

"They'll finish cooking without you," Macklin murmured. He looked down at Jordan's tense forehead and bent to kiss that too. "Relax, young Jordan. You didn't do all this by yourself."

"I led the way."

"Sh." Jordan's eyes bored into his as he slid one hand away from Jordan's and used it to smooth nitrile-covered fingers over Jordan's lips. "You take too much on yourself here. I'll talk about it after breakfast. But right now, you have a whole supportive *thing* going on in the kitchen and dining room, and people who very much want to be there for you. You're lucky, Jordan. I've never had that. Use it."

Jordan's intensity remained, but his eyes perceptibly changed focus.

"Where did you grow up, third son of a third son?"

Macklin grimaced. "You remember that, do you?"

"I've never had anybody throw their lineage in my face before."

Oh lord. "Wizards and grand witches tend to gather in compounds like those scary militia people, except you never hear of wizards and grand witches. They just own big houses and keep to themselves. In a way, it's sort of like here, except we hire housekeepers and cooks and stuff and, well, we tend to be really full of ourselves, so it's no fun at all."

Jordan did a slow blink, but he didn't pull his hand away. "There's a lot you're not telling me," he deduced. "You make it sound like prison."

"Felt that way growing up," Macklin said on a sigh. He smiled a little. "Wasn't breakfast with friends."

"We do this at least once a week," Jordan murmured. "We started in college, meeting for coffee. Cully always makes the most awful sweet coffee drink concoctions, and we all used to find ways to dump them down the sink when he wasn't looking because we didn't want to fall asleep after the sugar crash hit." He sighed, deflating a little, and Macklin caught hold of his hand as it tried to slide out of his grasp. "I sort of miss them now. I'd give about anything to have one of those super sweet dessert coffee drinks for breakfast."

"We'll get them back," Macklin promised rashly. He should know better. Just because he was pretty sure he knew what had happened did *not* mean he could fix it. What was happening in this tiny corner of the world was huge and dangerous and sort of terrifying—Josh's comment on the weather had cemented it—and Macklin *should* be reporting this directly to his father and the wizard council for the western states.

But they would come rushing in and grill Jordan and his friends and humiliate them and—what was worse—probably strip them of their powers, when it wasn't their fault at all. Everything that was wrong with wizards, from Macklin's point of view, was what would happen to this tiny group of people who had created the warm, welcoming kitchen and the table where you had to tell the truth.

Macklin wanted to protect them from that if he could.

"Thanks," Jordan murmured. He tugged on his hand again, and this time Macklin let him go, a little sad at the loss of contact. He stripped off the gloves and rewashed his hands, and then made use of the moisturizer on the side of the sink. He held his hands to his nose and inhaled, then looked at the label.

Kate's Boudoir—Teak and Marble

"Kate made this?" he asked, remembering Simon had said they all sold things at Bartholomew's stall.

"I distilled the oil," Jordan said. "Although"—and his lean mouth twisted—"I guarantee that no marbles were harmed in its making."

Macklin grinned at him, pleased. "Good to hear," he said solemnly. "All products should be so humane." He held his hands up to his nose again. "This has been... blessed. So much so that I almost can't smell the original oils. This was you and Kate. It's... masculine—very charged with action." He wrinkled his nose. "I sound like a perfume commercial, but that's what you were aiming at, right?"

Jordan nodded. "Yes. I mean, that's what I was hoping for in the scent, and we both do an invocation to bless the work. I do the oils; she mixes the lotions and soaps. I do the same thing with Cully's sachets. I guess it's how we all work. Even Bartholomew, although we didn't realize it until recently."

"You guys are lucky," Macklin said. "Your love for each other, your willingness to work together, to be a co-op as well as a coven, I think it might be what saved you here." He looked away from his hands—and that delicious, Jordan-y smell—and watched as Jordan's shoulders straightened and some of the defeat bled out of him. Goddess, he was a stunning man, younger than Macklin, but so self-assured. The mantle of authority that his father had spent his entire life trying to force Macklin to assume seemed to settle on Jordan's shoulders like it had been fitted for him. He didn't like the weight and probably didn't like the color, but he would wear it and he would use it and he would do justice to it because by Goddess it was *his*!

"I know good people," Jordan said simply, standing, apparently ready to venture back into the world and slay dragons.

Macklin couldn't help himself—he moved into Jordan's space and looked up—*up*—into that narrow, angular face.

"You recruited good people," he said throatily. "You surrounded yourself with good people, because you don't attract fools."

"What are you doing?" Jordan asked gently, like he was going to turn Macklin down. "Is this standard when you're called in to help a coven of feckless hedge witches? You move in on the available witch for shits and giggles?"

Macklin narrowed his eyes. "I've never been summoned to help anybody before," he said. "Hedge witches don't come to wizards for help because wizards are fascist assholes who will wipe out a coven in order to get rid of a teeny problem that could be fixed with a little bit of elbow grease and some kindness. I think the only reason you *did* get me is because you're such a bunch of sweet little bunnies who got stuck out in the rain that the magic came searching for the last wizard on earth who would turn you in. So thank your lucky stars—quite literally— that I'm the one who showed up."

He huffed out a breath and realized that Jordan's eyes had widened in alarm. "They'd wipe us out?" he squeaked.

Macklin winced. "They'd cast a binding," he said, hating that this was true. "On all of you, so you couldn't practice magic again. It's not fair—it's why hedge witches have traditionally hidden from wizards, probably since the first grandmother picked up a broom and told it to sweep. But... but your spell asked for help, and it was such an... innocent thing to ask for. You wanted to fix things for your friends. I mean, I've met you all. You're so... so damned pure, I guess. So you got me. I *am* the third wizard son of a third wizard son, but I haven't been home in seventeen years, because *fuck* those people. It… it wasn't a pleasant way to grow up."

He didn't want to talk about the training, the incessant lessons, the lack of joy in his household. His mother had been chosen for her lineage as the wife to the Sorcerer Direct, and he had been all but bred like a good racehorse.

Except unlike a good racehorse, he'd jumped the gate and gone tearing off into the wild blue the moment he'd been old enough to go to college. He'd gotten his degree in structural engineering and had lived his life working hard and playing hard and only doing magic if he damned well felt like it.

Getting jerked through that portal had felt like getting jerked out of the swimming pool and onto a bicycle, but now that he'd figured out where he was going, he didn't mind that the bicycle had gotten him here faster, because it turns out, there were some things you never forget.

But while Macklin had been wandering memory lane, Jordan's face had hardened, and his eyes went shiny and hurt.

"Great," he muttered. "Great. So if we don't figure out how to help our friends, the people who will come in and clean up after us might take away the one thing we have that can help them?"

Macklin nodded. "Yeah. Because I don't think they could rescue your friends, but I think you all can."

"Why?" Jordan asked suspiciously.

"Because," Macklin said—and he hadn't stepped out of Jordan's personal space yet because damn, he *had* lived and played hard, and he had enjoyed every minute of it. But Jordan Bryne was a whole new category of *play*… and *live*! "I think you and your friends have forged a very strong tie with one another. I've met hedge witches since I've left the compound, and that's one of their strengths that wizards don't acknowledge. The emotional ties you forge when your life isn't all about power and control—that's very powerful. I think your coven can save your friends when the wizards would sort of write them off as collateral damage. I think it's worth a try."

Jordan swallowed. His face was still hard, but his shiny, hurt eyes were just a little wider.

"But why are you standing so close?" he asked hoarsely, and Macklin raised his hand to cup Jordan's cheek again.

"Because, kid, you are like the literal hurricane. You have this energy in you. You've turned your friends into a force to be reckoned with, and I am not immune."

Jordan's eyes narrowed. "I told you last night, I don't have the time or the concentration for this." He caught Macklin's hand with his newly healed one, and Macklin looked at it, checking again for only the faintest scar.

Jordan saw the direction of his eyes, and crescents of red appeared on his cheeks.

Macklin smiled, knowing he was being an ass and not caring. "You felt it," he said, nodding. "Healing can be really sexy if it's done right, and you felt it!"

Jordan licked his lips. "I told you—" he began doggedly, but Macklin was done listening to his words when his eyes were saying something completely different.

"Just let me taste," he begged, sticking his face in the hollow of Jordan's neck and breathing in. They'd both used the same body wash that morning, but ah....

It smelled so much better on Jordan's body. "One taste." He moved up to run his nose along Jordan's long jaw.

"What happens then?" Jordan asked, sounding distracted indeed.

"Maybe we want another," Macklin murmured, and then he was there. Jordan's lips.

On the physical plane, their mouths touched, their breath mingled, and Macklin teased the seam of Jordan's lips gently with his tongue.

Behind Macklin's eyes, things were even more exciting than that. Fireworks, crashing waves, a hurricane of breathless longing: all of it made his palms tingle to touch more, made him want to plunder.

"Do we?" Macklin asked, his breath coming quicker.

"Want more?" Jordan asked, sounding equally as breathless.

"Yes, please," Macklin begged, and Jordan slid his palm up Macklin's chest and cupped his throat in the vee of his thumb and forefinger, holding Macklin in place just... so.

And with that, Jordan took the lead and plundered *him*.

Macklin opened his mouth, as surprised as a virgin, and let Jordan Bryne take him. His tongue swept in, his mouth claimed, as intense and masterful in kissing as he was chopping vegetables or defending his coven. Macklin responded, stunned at the ferocity of the kiss, at the wanting, at the raw power of it.

Macklin was usually the stalker. He'd never been prey before.

What a surprise to find he didn't want to run *anywhere*.

The kisses continued, hard but not punishing, breathless, wanting, sending Macklin into a dizzy spiral of needing to *give*.

He kissed back, he touched, rucking up Jordan's sweatshirt, reveling in the smooth skin and long, taut muscle underneath. This was a man who cleared out gardens and probably ran when he could. This was someone with ground-eating strides and longer sight and vision.

Jordan backed him up against the sink and pressed their bodies together, and through two sets of track pants, Macklin could feel the size and hardness of both of their erections. Goddess, there was plenty of dick for everybody there, wasn't there?

A thump on the door had Jordan ripping away his mouth, and Mack pressed a whimper into the side of his neck.

"J!" called Kate's boyfriend. "Table's set. We're waiting on you. Have you bled to death? Is that it? You bled to death and the new guy doesn't want to tell us?"

Macklin felt Jordan's rough chuckle through the skin of his throat, an unbelievably intimate vibration that made Macklin want to spend an eternity kissing him under his jaw.

"It's all healed," Jordan called. "If we're nice, maybe the new guy will teach us the spell." He offered Macklin a sweet kiss on the temple and then stepped away. After giving himself a quick glance in the mirror, he wiped his mouth on the shoulder of his sweatshirt, and opened the door, ostensibly to leave Macklin behind to clean up the first-aid supplies.

What Macklin really needed to do was make sure his knees were not, indeed, water.

Damn.

Macklin took stock of his face in the mirror and tried to pull his shit together. He was cheerfully pansexual and—unlike Jordan—had taken people up on their offers of threesomes and moresomes and never looked back. If he was breaking away from the wizarding compound and their restrictive "breeding" program that did *not* include same-sex couplings, he was going to do it in style! That had been his mantra going away to school, and he'd kept it up as he'd established job credentials in the everyday, nonmagical world and kept them. His colleagues knew he worked hard and played hard, and he made it very, very clear that he was not in it for the long haul.

But God, he'd never been kissed like that.

Like the person doing the kissing had the wherewithal to reach into his chest, pull out his heart, and either cup it in his hands and cherish it like a fragile thing…

Or stomp on it as it shattered into pieces.

"Stupid," he muttered. Stupid. Jordan was hot, a stellar attraction from long body to knife-blade features and even his lean, hard mouth. For someone younger than Macklin by nearly ten years, he had amazing self-possession, and his dedication to his coven made him seem much older. But he was a hedge witch. Stronger than ordinary, perhaps, but when all was said and done, there could be nothing about him that would turn Macklin's head to do anything other than leave when this was all over.

He caught another glimpse of himself in the mirror as he was turning away—hooded eyes, swollen lips, hectic flush—and wondered if virgins looked more or less debauched on their wedding nights.

One more swallow. One more deep breath. He had to go into that room and explain to the people there that their coven—and their lives—were about to change, and that there was some magic that should never be called upon.

That should have been more important than a kiss in the bathroom, but he was having a hard time believing it, even as he finally left.

I Can't Get No Satisfaction

"THE apple crumble was excellent," Jordan said, pushing back from the table a little. The frittata, the crumble, and the croissants had all added up to the kind of repast the lot of them had grown used to in the past three years. Finding a way to live close to each other had been one of the best things Jordan and his friends had done.

Bartholomew rapped gently on the table and winked. "And that's a review you can trust," he said, and the rest of the table laughed.

"It really was amazing," Macklin said from Jordan's right. "I, uh, didn't make a very good impression last night. Thanks for feeding me into submission."

More laughter, and Jordan nodded approvingly. Macklin looked… well, as delicious as breakfast had been, really. He'd been something the night before, his eyes flashing, his cheeks hot with indignation. But after hearing their story and listening, really listening, to their worry, the wizard had softened toward them, and Jordan might not have to kill him when this was over.

Which didn't say much about what Jordan *really* wanted to do to him while it was still going on.

But Jordan was determined not to think about that. He couldn't. There were too many important things to worry about.

"So," Jordan said when the silence had stretched long enough to ensure everybody was ready, "Macklin, do you have any ideas for what we should do next?"

Macklin gave him an unhappy look. "Well," he said, "first, I do need to go next door and have a word with your friends."

A lot of uncomfortable breaths whispered through people's noses.

"I'll take you." Jordan said it and thought he would be the only one, but when he glanced around, he realized that his whole coven—including Lachlan and Simon—had said it too.

"*I'll* take you," Jordan repeated, but he nodded at everybody, letting them know he appreciated the offer.

"Actually," Macklin said, biting his lip in a show of cautiousness, "it might be better if you let someone else do it. For one thing, you need to clear the garden. You told me so yourself, and it's a big job."

"I'll help with that, bruh," Josh said, offering a fist for the bumping. Jordan didn't leave him hanging, because Josh was solid like that.

"Thanks," Jordan said.

"I can too," Kate offered, but Macklin shook his head.

"Kate, I'm going to need you and Bartholomew when I'm done checking out next door, I think. I have an idea, and I'm going to need a potions master and someone who can make potions and oils accessible. Alex, I may need you to do some actual accounting for me and to help me look stuff up in the library." He glanced at Lachlan and Simon and smiled charmingly. "And if you two are volunteering, I'd love to have your help as well."

"Sure," Lachlan said, but Simon was a little more circumspect. Of course, he should have been at work, so he had to be careful with his time.

"What are we going to be doing?"

Macklin grimaced. "Well, if next door is what I think it is, you're all going to be doing it."

Jordan stared at him, his stomach suddenly in knots. "Doing what?" he asked dryly.

"Moving."

The table erupted into chaos, and all those pleasant thoughts Jordan had been having about Macklin Quintero evaporated in an instant.

TWO hours later, Jordan's bare chest was running with sweat as he ripped a stripped tomato plant out of the ground and heaved it toward the pile of dead vegetation. He gave a healthy scream of outrage as he did it, and Josh did the same thing from the corn rows.

He wasn't sure how the others were dealing with the bomb Macklin had dropped that morning, but he had to admit that butchering an already dead garden had some serious magic in terms of catharsis.

With a growl, he attacked the next tomato plant, yanking with all his strength because the roots were in deep. His arm muscles bulged, his back strained, and when it finally gave way, it felt like a skeleton releasing its bony fingers around its most treasured possession. He roared in triumph and heaved the plant onto the pile, barely missing Macklin as he approached the two of them from around the front.

"Whoa!" Macklin shouted, jumping back.

"Fuck," Jordan snarled before remembering that this *wasn't* Macklin's fault, and nobody—Jordan especially—had the right to take out his ire on the wizard they had apparently snatched out of midair and dropped into their problems.

"Sorry," Jordan panted, and Josh came out, also bare-chested and sweating, from behind the remaining cornstalks and chuckled.

"Dude!" Josh said.

"Yeah, I'm sorry, Macklin," Jordan repeated. "I didn't see you."

"You almost clobbered him with the tomato plant! Epic!"

Jordan grimaced. "Clumsy," he amended, trying to calm down. "I truly didn't mean to throw that at you." He noticed Macklin's pale features and set jaw. "Especially after how you must have spent the last hour."

"Dude," Josh said in apology. "So sorry, man. That's the worst."

Macklin nodded in agreement. He'd spent the morning with Dante and Cully, and Jordan was well aware it hadn't gotten any better in that house since they'd first disappeared.

"It's… every bit as bad as you all said it was," Macklin admitted. "I… they were there, Bartholomew introduced me as a friend, and they took turns appearing in the room to talk and then disappearing. Sometimes I could hear their voices and not see them, and sometimes they were just drifting through walls."

Jordan shuddered. He'd been there. Watching his old friends caught in that limbo, and so, so unaware of what they were missing about the lives they were trying to live. It broke his heart every time.

"I'm sorry," he said for the fifth time in as many minutes. But this time it meant something different.

"No," Macklin said. "I'm sorry. I sort of wrecked your world this morning, and none of this is your fault."

Jordan grunted, not wanting to talk about it but knowing he had no choice.

"Here," he said, pointing to the porch, which sported a camp chair in the shade. "Come talk to me and Josh while we keep pulling shit out. We've cleared all the veggies—" He indicated a harvest basket only half-full of the last of the tomatoes and the squash, as well as some green beans. "—but we need to get everything to the pile for a bonfire tonight."

"Not Samhain?" Macklin asked, eyes sharpening.

"Well, ordinarily, yes," Jordan said. "But we'd already figured we'd need to have a big ritual of sorts. We'd planned to use Simon's and Lachlan's properties, because together, both lots form a five-pointed star. We were going to put the bonfire in the middle, but first we were going to ask you for help."

"Really?" Macklin said, eyes big.

Jordan stared at him. "Were we wrong?"

"No. In fact, how much property, again?"

Jordan gave him a grim look, because this had surprised the entire group. "Ninety-nine acres," he said levelly.

"Damn, son. That's some coincidence!"

Jordan grimaced. "So was being given a witch's cottage when so many of us were at least decently talented in the magic department." He let out a breath. "Or do you think that was planned too?"

Macklin picked up the camp chair and moved it down the porch and a little closer to where Jordan and Josh were working. "Maybe someday Helen will come back and tell us," he muttered, "but I doubt she has that much personal responsibility."

Jordan paused in the act of massacring another plant, this one zucchini squash. "Do you really think she meant to leave us with a…." He glanced around and found he couldn't say it—not on this particular plot of ground. "A presence?"

Macklin sighed and sank down into the chair like he was close to falling down instead. "I have no idea," he said.

Jordan's arms ached and his head ached and his back ached—and his heart ached—because no matter how much yelling at dead plants he and Josh had done, it hadn't made anything Macklin had told them that morning less logical.

According to Macklin, those who practiced witchcraft didn't have "demons" in the classical sense, but they did have presences that had the same effect. Sort of the worst of human nature gone to seed so long it took root and grew.

Some of the same suspects materialized among magical folks as existed among the nonmagical—apathy and entropy made an appearance, much like sloth and gluttony did among ordinary people. Pride was apparently a bad thing all around, as were vanity and greed. There were different ones too, however. Apparently the demons of self-destruction and abnegation were fairly common, as was the demon of shame.

In this case, the demon of abnegation had been in the cul-de-sac long before Jordan and his friends had arrived.

Helen's cottage, devoted to her craft and her familiars, did not, in fact, hold any other indicators of the woman who'd lived there. Macklin had quizzed them all after breakfast, and what they'd told him—she was an older woman who liked sixties music and wore T-shirts with often riotous slogans on them—didn't reveal much about her. Had she had lovers? Children? A coven?

Since she'd left, not a soul had come asking for her. Even her mail was generic.

"She let the things she wanted slip away," Macklin said softly. "Apparently her first act of rebellion against becoming, I don't know, a part of this house, the feeder of cats, and perpetrator of the garden, was hopping on that motorcycle and driving away. She probably thought she could come back after a vacation or something but…." He shook his head.

"Once she left she saw what had been missing from her life," Jordan deduced. He had wondered, getting sucked into the house's needy vortex, what exactly it would take to break out of that stranglehold of responsibility imposed upon him and his friends.

Desertion seemed to be the answer. But it didn't sit well; not well at all.

Jordan went after another squash plant with ferocity, fighting with all his might the roots that should have been long dead.

He pulled the plant out with a grunt, grateful for his work gloves and ignoring the chafing of the leaves against his arms as he snarled in fury until the damned thing was out. He looked at the roots in frustration, noting that some of them had broken off, and wondered if this plant would be back again next year.

Well, probably. Wasn't that how volunteers happened?

But was it a good plant? Was it steeped in abnegation or whatever? Would eating it cause him and his people to sublimate their desires again and again and again until they lost their humanity and personality entirely and became vessels for pure magic?

"Stop," Macklin said mildly, and Jordan became aware he'd been staring at the squash plant for an inordinately long time.

"Stop what?" Jordan asked as he tossed the thing onto the pile.

"Stop obsessing about what you did or thought that was wrong."

"You just told me that my cul-de-sac was being taken over by a presence or a demon or whatever, and I'm the one that fed the damned thing exactly what it wanted!" Gah! That burned. His entire life he'd been taught to be humble and grateful for the gifts he'd been given, and he'd lived by that. One of the reasons he'd loved his friends so very much was that they seemed to be driven by that same belief that you took your talents and made them into something that pleased humanity. It was such a simple idea. But under his leadership, he and his friends had cast a spell that forced them to voice the thing they wanted most in the world, and their self-effacement had been exactly what the presence had needed to unleash hell on the lot of them.

"Self-deprecation isn't normally a problem, Jordan." Macklin sounded as compassionate now as he had when he'd explained the whole thing after breakfast that morning. That didn't erase the fact that, in order to stop feeding the presence, Jordan and his coven needed to not only leave it, but raze the houses and thresholds that gave it shelter and allowed it to grow.

"It shouldn't be," Jordan said bitterly. Dammit, he *liked* his friends and their cheerful lack of arrogance or conceit.

"In fact," Macklin continued, his voice stern, "the world would be a better place if the right people had it. But the people in this cul-de-sac *aren't* the right people. Imagine if Bartholomew became too consumed with magic to bake. Or Kate and Josh forgot about that fantastic relationship they have and became all about what their parents wanted—"

"Dude," Josh said from behind what was left of the rows of corn. "Fate worse than death!"

Jordan had to laugh. "Yeah. I hear you. Moderation. Wanting to be sustained isn't a sin—gluttony is a problem. Being happy you've accomplished something isn't bad. Being too proud to admit you're wrong or you need help can wreak devastation. The problem isn't that we're humble. It's that the burden of humility was crushing down the thing that makes us... *us*."

With a defeated sigh, he started kicking at the roots of another deeply entrenched squash plant.

"I have no idea how I'm going to tell my dads that we have to move out of here because of a paranormal infestation."

"Don't sweat it," Josh said, and Jordan had a moment to be grateful that Josh's general good nature seemed to have given him some immunity to the presence that had infected their cul-de-sac. Yeah, sure, when asked to put his heart's desire into a spell, he got caught up in the wording, but in his everyday dealings?

Josh Hernandez spoke nothing but the truth and had no problems with anybody knowing he was perfectly comfortable in his own general Josh-ness.

"Don't sweat it?" Jordan asked, shivering a little in the breeze. When he was in full rampage mode, it was definitely too hot for a shirt, but now that they'd slowed down a little, well, his nipples were pebbling.

"Yeah, don't sweat it." Josh shrugged. "Tell Sebastian straight out, and he'll be here to paint the house, the birds, the whole thing. And then he'll get all excited about how we're haunted by crushing humility, and Asa will raise his eyebrows and do whatever Sebastian tells him. And in the meantime, your grandmother will cook for us—which, honestly, is really what I'm looking for here—so, you know, if you could throw in a word for me, I love that bacon cabbage stuff she makes."

He smiled winningly, and Jordan laughed a little, reaching for the shirt that was hanging over the porch railing.

"No, no," Macklin said with a twist of his lips. "Feel free to leave it off."

Jordan stared at him, and in that moment, their entire interlude in the bathroom came flooding back, and he threw the shirt on hurriedly because he felt the flush invade his back, his chest, his neck—

"Your ears!" Josh crowed. "Oh my God, J. I've never seen your ears do that unless you're drinking vodka or something. Dang. Did you forget sunblock?"

Jordan shook his head, because with his coloring, he *never* forgot sunblock, even though he managed to tan nicely once he built up some tolerance for the sun in the spring.

"Wait, no!" Josh gasped. "It's on your neck now too. Macklin, is this some sort of evil house demon or something? Do we have to perform an exorcism? Is he gonna turn that color everywhere?"

"I hope so," Macklin said, those piercing blue eyes twinkling unmercifully. "I'll be so disappointed not to find out."

"Grown-ups learn to live with disappointment," Jordan said dryly, not wanting to think about it. Goddess, his friends were trapped and had been for far too long, and now that Macklin was here, he'd given them a directive, and Jordan was going to need his full concentration to carry it out. No time—*no time*—to get involved in a new relationship, even if it was just for the duration of the crisis.

"Yes, but well-rounded witches learn to give in to temptation," Macklin purred, and Jordan scowled at him.

"We're not having this conversation now," Jordan said primly, bending over to get a grip on the plant he'd kicked into submission.

"We'll have it sometime," Macklin promised, but Jordan didn't think so.

"Josh!" Jordan called. "You and Kate up to having Macklin in the guest room tonight?"

Josh had decimated the last of the corn, but apparently that hadn't affected his hearing one iota.

"No, Jordan," he said, sounding like a teacher talking to a fractious child. "Kate and I are trying to make a baby."

Jordan gave him his best "Oh, come on!" expression, but Josh read that too.

"You guys have things to discuss. Maybe naked. Dude, I'm saying. If you want to get out of that whole abnegatory thing, this guy's a place to start."

"He's right here, traitor," Jordan said, voice flat. He didn't even want to look at Macklin.

Josh rolled his eyes and dumped the corn on the pile, then grabbed a shovel and strode to the potato and carrot beds. "Man, you haven't told him what your wish was. Don't think I haven't noticed. This whole thing started 'cause you got your heart stomped on, and instead of wishing for a date with a pretty anybody, you asked for—"

Jordan held up his hand in exasperation. "Do we have to right now?" he begged.

"Fine," Josh muttered, standing on the shovel and pushing down. "But don't think this isn't gonna come back to bite us in the—*oh my God, that's gross!*"

Jordan and Macklin rushed over to see hundreds of potato bugs erupting out of the hole Josh had carved. With a surprisingly high-pitched scream, Josh leapt out of the bed, and they all watched as the earth shifted away from a seething mass of the things, which were threatening to crawl out of the potato bed and infiltrate the entire garden, if not the neighborhood.

Jordan growled low in his throat, and the spell ripped out of him with a surge of anger.

Bug of blight
Quit my sight
Come to harm
In the starling swarm
Ravens feed
So these bugs don't breed
Turkeys eat

On their flesh so sweet
Birds come down
And clear this ground!
So mote it be!

When he said the last line, he heard Josh and Macklin chanting it with him, and he felt a surge of gratitude for their help.

And then he and Macklin and Josh all heard the beating of wings.

"Oh fudgedoodles," Josh muttered, and Macklin and Jordan both screamed, "*Run!*"

They barely made it through the back door before the swarm of birds descended.

JORDAN paced the house, a spray bottle of sage and frankincense oil mixed with deionized water in his hand. He stopped at every windowsill and doorframe, reciting, "Protect this space from harm and violence," and rubbing his finger in the spray spatter to make a rune of safety as he went.

Macklin sat at the kitchen table, making them sandwiches because apparently Jordan and Josh had worked until nearly three in the afternoon, and it was lunchtime. Josh was on his cell phone comforting Kate, who was across the cul-de-sac with Alex, Simon, Bartholomew, and Lachlan. They'd been searching through spell books trying to find a spell that would purify, protect, and seal the space of the cul-de-sac once they left it.

They'd *all* heard the birds descending, and had peered out their window to see the backyard of the witch's cottage looking like an Alfred Hitchcock movie, and Kate's nearly hysterical call had pretty much followed the slamming of the door.

Jordan and Josh had ignored it and run throughout the house, spelling all the points of entry with basic protection, until Jordan came to the front door and stuck his head out, searching anxiously for his furry sentinels.

He found the front lawn guarded by the Nine, every animal on high alert in the cat version of parade rest, eyes scanning the skies. At one point, a starling swooped too low, and the tiny, light-boned calico cat made a seven foot—Jordan would swear to it—leap into the air to take the poor thing down with a savage bite to its spine.

Jordan gently closed the door before he could see what happened next and spelled the threshold with extra fervency.

As the door shut, he heard Macklin's voice raised in a Latin chant and felt an amazingly strong ripple of power encase the walls, and for a moment, they all gave a sigh of relief.

Then, finally, Josh could answer his phone.

He and Kate had been talking for the last half hour. Jordan's windows had been pelted with tomatoes after they'd closed the back door, so they couldn't see the state of the bird cloud. Kate helped keep them updated, but he could hear the thread of panic in her voice even through the phone Josh held to his ear.

She needed her mate, and Jordan couldn't blame her.

With a sigh he went rooting through the hall closet, relieved to see that a few of the ten umbrellas he'd first bought when this whole thing had started remained at his house, although the others had been scattered among the rest of the coven.

"What are you doing?" Macklin asked.

"Blue for protection," Jordan murmured, spraying the umbrella with his bottle. Frankincense he liked, but the smell of sage had never been one of his favorites. Still....

Umbrella bold
Keep the one who holds
This safe from harm.
Endure this charm
In the face of birds
And magic words
And all that seek
Havoc to wreak
In love's name and the Goddess's blessing we pray
So mote it be.

Josh and Macklin were a beat behind this time, but that was probably because the rhyme was a little rusty.

"*So mote it be*," they both said.

"Here," Macklin said. "Give it to me."

Jordan wasn't aware of how much he'd come to depend on Macklin's confident presence and the bare wealth of power that rumbled under him like the motor of his well-tuned motorcycle until he handed over the thing he was hoping would protect Josh from the birds while he ran across the cul-de-sac to Kate.

Macklin took it and said his own spell, this one in Latin, and even Josh gasped as he felt the magic move. Together they watched as the umbrella's plain blue fabric began to shine, glowing with gold and silver, throwing off sparklets of power.

They both looked at Josh, who said into the phone, "Hang on, babe. I'll be right over," before pressing End Call and sliding the phone into the pocket of his jeans.

Jordan realized numbly that Josh was still shirtless—but since his shirt had been left in the garden, hanging over the wheelbarrow, he assumed Josh was going to write off one ratty concert T-shirt without a single glance back.

"Be careful," Jordan said. "And hurry."

"And let us know if there's any of those hideous devil bugs in the cul-de-sac," Macklin said with so much revulsion that Jordan and Josh stared.

"They're Jerusalem crickets," Jordan said blankly. "They're sort of a marvel of engineering."

"They're gross, J," Josh told him. "I know you like bugs and shit, but that's gonna give me bad dreams. Saying. I wish it had been regular crickets."

"Regular crickets are better?" Macklin asked, and Josh shrugged.

"They're sort of shiny and armored, and they do that thing with their back legs. Ask J—he'll tell you. It's very cool. These bugs had fat squishy heads." He shuddered. "Don't question which bugs are gonna give me nightmares, J. Believe me, I know."

"Understood," Jordan said, loving his friend a lot in that moment. "Go fast, let us know if any bugs got out, and don't bother the Nine—they're busy."

Josh nodded. "Hear ya. I'll call as soon as I get there. Spell the threshold when I go." With that, they bumped foreheads and Josh grabbed the umbrella. "Ooh! It's vibrational!" he said happily before stepping outside of the house and opening it up.

Jordan spent a moment watching him run down the path to the driveway, noting that a few birds came out to harry him, but not the entire flock. He hurriedly shut the door before the birds spotted him and went in for the kill—dead birds were really unlucky, and if the last few weeks had taught him anything, it was that free-floating bad karma hurt really bad when it bit you on the ass.

When the door was closed and resealed, Jordan put his back to it and slid down to sit, hugging his knees. His phone rang in his pocket, and he pulled it out, seeing Josh's text and relaxing a little more.

Made it. Barty's been baking. It's diabetes central here. Think we could get a pizza delivery through the birds? Never mind. Lachlan's brought a turkey. Come over when it's safe, kk?

Kk, Jordan sent back, smiling a little at Josh's foolishness.

He set the phone in his lap and leaned his head against the door, closing his eyes a little. "Josh is safe," he said quietly.

To his surprise, Macklin slid down the door with him and handed him a tuna sandwich wrapped in a paper towel.

"Eat," he said gently.

"Sure." Jordan took a bite and munched with determination. Food was fuel, right?

"This wasn't your fault," Macklin told him.

"Sure it was."

"Well, maybe a little. You do know you were feeding into the demon when the bugs showed up."

Jordan had to force his next swallow. "I was *what*?"

"Let's see," Macklin said. "I was flirting with you, and you were shutting me down—"

"Because we need to be practical," Jordan told him, forehead wrinkled.

"Sure. And then Josh spoke up, because apparently he has the wisdom of the gods in the body of a granite quarry, and he said hey, why shouldn't you guys be discussing things naked."

"He's a nice guy," Jordan said with dignity. "He was going to get laid tonight, Alex and Barty were probably going to get laid tonight, and he wanted everybody to be happy. That doesn't mean it was a good idea."

Something thudded off the back door, probably a bird, and Jordan winced. Goddammit.

"And then he said—and this is true—that you hadn't told me what your one wish was, the one that magic had pulled out of you as truth, and I realized that, hey, very sneaky on your part, but he was *right.* You're the worst one of the lot, and that includes Bartholomew."

"Bartholomew was afraid of getting his heart stomped on," Jordan retorted. "That's valid. I just wanted...." He let out a sigh and thunked his head back against the door again.

"What?" Macklin asked. "Come on, Jordan. We've got eruptions of bugs and a plague of birds and holy fucknuggets—what's it going to take?"

"I told them," Jordan said. "I ponied up to the people who mattered, the people I wronged. Why do you have to know?"

"So I don't matter?" Macklin's voice went soft and hurt.

Jordan blew out a breath. "Of course you matter. We yanked you by the back of the neck and said, 'Help us!' and you said, 'Sure, and while I'm at it, I'm gonna save you from my awful family who would help you right out of this thing you really love too.' Of course you matter. This is just…." He rubbed his chest, feeling helpless and mute.

Macklin covered his hand, moving close enough to rest his head on Jordan's shoulder.

"Come on, Jordan," Macklin murmured. "What's it going to cost to let one more person into your little circle?"

"You're the third in a month," Jordan muttered. "And I know that sounds like I'm splitting hairs, but I'm not. My friends are special. I… I was so lonely when I was a kid. It got better after Sebastian showed up—he's sort of an extrovert, and Josh is right, he makes everything better—but I'm a little autistic, diagnosed, and a little OCD—that's speculation—and moderately ADHD, but I haven't needed medication for it since I hit college. And what all of that equals is that I hyperfocus on shit, and I get super intense, and I'm a social nightmare, and that makes people *really* uncomfortable around me. And all of my friends— every one of them—looked at me and saw something that made them go, 'Hey, I'm gonna follow this guy out to the river and take pictures of bugs!' You don't find that in everybody, and I've never taken it for granted."

He heard Macklin's indrawn breath and waited for him to recoil, pull back, withdraw in some way that indicated Jordan was, per usual, just a little too *Jordan* to deal with. His father and Sebastian and his Aunt Bella had all been so good at dealing with him like a normal little kid, and then a normal teenager, treating his medication regimen like putting on a pair of glasses, and lessons in social behavior like they were as normal as a math tutor—something Jordan had never needed.

Once Jordan had gotten to college and been able to control his environment, his social interactions, and the people he was grouped with, all those problems that haunted him in high school and middle school had evaporated. He'd even managed to get laid semiregularly, and that had been pretty amazing too.

But building his circle of friends had taken trust, confidence, and a sort of faith he'd never been able to find in himself when looking for a lover.

Maybe that's why he hadn't wished for love when he'd been overcoming a broken heart. He'd been convinced that this was one thing he was never going to have.

Macklin's head stayed right where it was, and he let that gasp out slowly.

"You going to take back our little moment in the bathroom now?" Jordan asked, not bitterly but because he liked to make sure of things.

"Goddess no," Macklin said fervently. "Kid, nothing you have done since I've met you has made me want you one iota less."

Jordan let out a snort. "I don't know what to do with that," he said honestly, but then he didn't know how else to be but honest. It was a failing. He'd been pretty hard-assed with Lachlan when Bartholomew had first brought him to the coven, because he'd watched Barty break his heart over Lachlan for nearly two years. Turns out Lachlan was the world's greatest guy, and he needn't have worried. Apparently super-overprotectiveness was some sort of syndrome too.

Macklin stayed right where he was, and for a moment they listened to the mayhem as a thousand birds met a million bugs.

"It's got to be easing up by now," Jordan said after a minute. The screeching of the birds seemed to be growing fainter, and no potato bugs had tried to crawl underneath the doorframe, for which Jordan was grateful. Not as grateful as Macklin or Josh, but grateful. They had a way of turning up in garbage disposals or drains, none of which was pretty.

"Why bugs?" Macklin asked, and even though the birds were dying down and they were sitting on the floor in front of the front door, he didn't seem inclined to move.

And Jordan? Jordan was so tired. Besides getting to bed at dark-thirty a.m. the night before, there had been the worry, the ever-present, constant worry, about what the neighborhood and the house were going to do next.

His friends couldn't spend every night on his couch. The music coming through the walls, the drafts, the voices—which didn't show up when other people were there—and the flickering lights all behaved themselves better when another person was in the house. But Jordan didn't want to impose that need on Alex or Barty or Josh or Kate too much, because it wasn't fair. It had been easier when Dante and Cully had been around to share the burden, but without them, Jordan was starting to realize how much the house, then neighborhood, was draining from everybody even before the spell.

It was just so peaceful there, sitting next to Macklin. And bugs were one of his favorite subjects.

"Bugs are perfect," Jordan said patiently. "Whatever a bug is designed for, every part of his anatomy, his nervous system, his skeleton, it's all designed for that purpose. Ants that leave chemical trails so they can smell their way along a path or caterpillars with their segmented bodies designed for metamorphosis—every part of a tiny bug is perfect. When we started studying Wicca, I thought about bugs because it's like the universe and the natural world and the seasons all interact together in synchrony, and bugs are a stellar microscopic example of that. And if you look at the world that way, it feels like everything will work in glorious concert if we just act kindly and have faith."

He took a breath, but Macklin was still listening, so he went on.

"That ant following his chemical trail is working for his hill. That caterpillar gorging himself on leaves knows that someday his world will look very different, and so will he. It's all... exactly as their genetic material and the universe ordained," Jordan said happily. "I even love my job. I'm a forensic entomologist, and I study the way bugs interact with organic matter to do things like determine time of death or where a subject has been or what's been done to it. And while the death itself is sad—often tragic—knowing the bugs were there to so perfectly return the mortal remains of someone back to the earth which gave this person birth... well, that seems special. It seems like proof that the afterlife is kind, since life here on earth is so particularly designed."

He finished talking and realized Macklin had pulled back and was gazing at him—staring—his blue eyes so dark they were almost black.

"What?" he asked, aware he'd been talking uninterrupted for what seemed like hours now.

Macklin pushed Jordan's hair out of his eyes, the gesture intimate and unobjectionable. "I spent my entire childhood learning magic," he said with a little bit of awe, "and not one adult could explain the magic of the earth and the circle of life and the interaction of creatures great and small as wonderfully as you just did. It makes me wish you could have taught *me* when I was a child, but...." His full mouth quirked slightly, and he threw his black hair out of his own eyes with a little toss of his head.

"But what?" Jordan asked.

"But I'd rather hear it from you as an adult, because it means my thoughts right now are perfectly appropriate."

Jordan had to glance away. "Did you not *just* hear me say I'm not good at relationships?"

Macklin's laugh brought his attention right back to that square-jawed, rough-stubbled face. "I heard you say that whatever you focus on gets 110 percent of your direct attention," Macklin corrected. He shuddered ecstatically. "Kid, that does *not* sound like a bad thing."

Jordan snorted softly. "Look around me," he said, nodding his chin to indicate the other houses on the cul-de-sac. "Look at where the other people in my life are, relationship-wise. What does that tell you about where *I* want to be?"

Macklin's gaze searched his. "Was that what you asked for when you gave up your word?"

"Yes and no," Jordan told him, completely truthful.

"Then what was your word?" Macklin pressed.

And Jordan had opened his mouth to say it—to give him the keys to his own soul, as it were—when Macklin's eyes widened.

"Fuck," he said, his full mouth parting slightly.

"What?"

"Oh Jesus. Kid, I'll be back as soon as I can."

"But where are you go—"

Macklin disappeared. Into thin air. Like a hologram or a mirage.

"—ing?" Jordan finished, all the air knocked out of his lungs. Outside, the sound of the birds had faded to normal, and tomatoes had stopped pelting the back porch. Inside, the cottage was silent, and over the tuna fish sandwich—most of which was still on the napkin in his hand—he could smell desert and sage and Macklin.

And the ever-so-faint tinge of sulfur.

People Got to be Free

WELL, *shit.*

Macklin felt it about two breaths before it happened—not enough time to really warn Jordan and not enough time to brace himself and make it stop.

In fact he had just enough time to be glad he was sitting on his ass because he fucking hated portals and he really hated the way the world seemed to spin when he went through one. Part of the reason he'd been so damned cranky when he'd stomped into Jordan's coven the night before—was it only the night before?—was that he *hated going through portals*.

And also, he'd almost dumped his motorcycle when he'd come through, and the adrenaline rush had been heinous.

Fortunately from the moment he'd felt the first tickle this time, he'd known where he was going.

The world stopped swimming around him, and he found himself seated on a three-thousand-dollar Persian rug done in black and silver—the moon from outer space. The rug was on a teakwood floor, and the furniture around it was also teak: heavy, stained dark, and oppressive as fuck.

As were the dark green tapestries on the teak-paneled walls.

He'd been gone from home for seventeen years, and God, one breath of the magic, the cold iron around the fireplace, and the incense his father burned during spellwork, and he was eighteen again, telling his old man to fuck off, and that he would rather live in the human world than in this goddamned prison for another moment.

And his father had let him go, promising direly that he'd be coming back of his own accord.

No.

Just… no.

"Macklin." The heavy bass/baritone was unmistakable, and Macklin met his father's piercing blue eyes with his own irritated stare.

Alistair Quintero appeared to be almost Macklin's mirror image—if Macklin had the lined face of thirty years in the future and had white streaks in his black, black hair. Also unlike Macklin, who occasionally didn't shave for a couple of days, Alistair had cultivated a beard in the last twenty years, but Macklin suspected that was because he was getting a little jowly. He'd always been damned vain of his good looks, proud that his three wives, or broodmares, depending on how one thought about it, had enjoyed their time in bed with him while they'd been producing children.

Macklin's mother had been his first wife, and as far as Macklin knew, she was still occupying the wives' wing of the great house. Macklin's father had his own bedroom, but he would have the wife of his choice visit when he was in the mood for that sort of thing.

In the human world, it would look very much like a cult. The only difference—and to Macklin's mind it wasn't much of one—was that the leaders, the wizards and grand witches, could actually do the magic they claimed.

The magic elephant in the room was that like any other form of power, whether money, influence, or talent, magic did not entitle people to claim superiority.

Macklin had said it. He'd said it a *lot*. And finally, he'd left because he was tired of saying it. The day he'd departed for college—without his father's blessing but with lots of scholarships from some amazing test scores and essays—was the last day he'd ever wanted to set foot here.

Which was why, perversely, he stayed on his ass for as long as possible after he'd been sucked back.

"The actual fuck," he said, wrapping his arms around his knees.

"You were in danger." Alistair glared at him from the summoning circle etched on the hearth.

"Beg to differ," Macklin said. "Send me back."

"Your crystal was darkened," Alistair thundered, gesturing to the game board on his desk. Macklin had seen it before, had been schooled in how to make one of his own. It featured stones set in proximity to each other on an etched map of the world in a way that appeared random, but Macklin knew better. Each stone, by color, intensity, and magical property, represented one of Alistair's sixteen children.

Macklin noticed that his own stone—a raw, unpolished chunk of lapis lazuli—had darkened from a deep sapphire blue to something richer, almost a purple-black, with streaks of gold studded through it. He studied the stone, holding his hand out almost absentmindedly and counting on his natural affinity with the rock that represented him to lead the material into his hand.

It landed with a satisfying smack, and he examined it carefully.

"Dark, yes," he said, running his fingers along the contours of the crystal. "But dark isn't automatically evil. Sometimes it's just secretive." Macklin stared up at his father. "You yanked me away from one of the best kisses I might have gotten in my life because I've matured enough to keep a goddamned secret? Have you *seen* your own rock? It started off as amber, Dad. I remember. Now it's *onyx*. Onyx doesn't even *do* anything but keep secrets. So fuck off if you don't like my stone color and let me go back to my kiss!"

It might not have been a kiss, Macklin was well aware. It might have been a confession. It might have been the one thing Jordan wanted above all others, which was fine, because then Macklin could decide if he could give Jordan that thing and *then* go get that kiss.

Goddess, Macklin hoped so.

Jordan Bryne's awkward, blurty confession had been one of the most dear things Macklin had ever heard. And one of the most awesome. Because Jordan, contrary to his own perceptions, wasn't any of his labels. He wasn't his atypicalities—"autistic" or "OCD" or "ADHD." He was *intense*. And that intensity was the thing that probably really attracted his friends. His friends in the coven saw that focus and that intellect and that capacity for caring, and that's why they were his coven. Because those things mattered to them too.

And Jordan's protectiveness made him so very, very… well, the antithesis of Macklin's father, for one thing, who would rather control than care.

"Son, if she's worth the kiss, you can bring her back to the compound." As though he were offering an olive branch, Macklin's father reached down to give Macklin a hand up.

Macklin ignored him and stood on his own. "He's definitely worth the kiss, and I'm not bringing him anywhere. He's got a home and a family, and they don't need your interference, thank you very much." He hoped his tongue didn't trip over the word "family" or his father hadn't heard the hesitation when Macklin thought "coven" instead. Oh, he may have been irritated, but it was *extremely* important that Macklin not drop any of Jordan's precious secrets right now.

"Macklin, it's high time you stopped this experiment of living with the humans and started a family. Your brothers have all given me grandchildren—"

"I did notice the board was brighter and more sparkly than before," Macklin said dryly. "You know, I do send letters. I have an address and a business and everything—"

"Which you're apparently neglecting since you didn't show up to work yesterday," his father growled.

Macklin rocked back on his heels. "You *monitored me*?" he asked, stunned. When he'd gone on his motorcycle ride the day before, he'd texted his work partner, Billy Parks, that he'd be taking the day off. Billy did the same thing, going to Reno sometimes to gamble—responsibly, and he showed Macklin his win/loss sheet to prove it, and Macklin took his own days off. Some days, he could freely admit, it was to get laid. Not so much in the last few years, but that was none of his father's business.

"I awoke this morning and saw the change in your stone, and I was *worried*," his father snarled. "For sixteen years that stone has flitted around the damned board, which is fine, but it never once showed any change, and now you've got secrets?"

"Dad, I left here so my entire life could *be* a secret! Maybe I finally found somebody else I wanted to keep secret from you too!" Because Goddess, the last thing he wanted was for his father to meet—and possibly demoralize and maybe destroy—the intense, talented, *magical* Jordan Bryne.

Alistair scowled. "There is obviously something bigger going on here than a romance with a young man."

"Not likely," Macklin said, and as he watched, the stone in his hand grew a little closer to that autumn sky blue. Well. Imagine that. It was more than the truth. He just had to remember that purity for the rest of this conversation.

His father noticed as well. "Really?" he asked, and for a moment—a bare moment—he sounded almost human in his disappointment. "A young man? How long have you known him?"

Macklin smiled, bemused. "Less than a day. And I'd like to get back and make that a little longer, if you don't mind." He closed his eyes and started centering himself, drawing on the remaining energy in the room for another portal. A part of him was really pissed, because portals were big magic, and they sucked a lot of energy out of even a skilled wizard for at least a week.

"Wait, Macklin!"

Macklin huffed out a breath. "What?"

He actually looked at his father, and saw—much to his surprise—hurt.

"That's it?" Alistair said. "I haven't seen you for years and you're just… going back?"

Macklin swallowed and found his throat surprisingly tight. "I left here seventeen years ago because I didn't like the way you ran things." He glanced around and held his hands up in a classic shrug. "The actual fuck, Alistair. What about any part of the last ten minutes makes me think you've changed?"

Alistair scowled. "I was making sure my son was not getting seduced by evil."

In his pocket, Macklin felt what must have been the sixteenth buzz, indicating Jordan was giving his own version of "the actual fuck" via text.

"My friend—the one who was maybe going to kiss me? He's doing this magical wonderful thing right now. You may have heard of it. He's using a *phone* to contact me. I'm not sure if you know this, but they make these tiny handheld pocket computers that *also* communicate. They had a version of them seventeen years ago, but trust me, they're gonna blow your mind now." He realized he was being a sarcastic ass, but his fury was not letting him back down.

"Would you have even answered me if I'd texted or called you?" Alistair demanded, and Macklin gave a bitter laugh.

"Well, not that you'll ever know now, but *yes*! I'm the idiot who's been sending Christmas cards and letters to my brothers with the expectation that somebody gave a damn, remember?"

That rankled him too. Josue, in particular, he'd been close to. Josue—the son of his father's second wife—had been a few years younger than Macklin and had seemed to need protection fiercely. Macklin had shared his departure with Josue alone, and Josue had kept his word and not told a soul that Macklin was leaving.

"It is possible," Alistair said, voice arid, "that your brothers did not receive your letters."

Macklin wasn't aware that he was even summoning power until the fireplace—which was always stocked with wood for just such an occasion—was suddenly hosting a rip-roaring bonfire.

Macklin had barely remembered to channel his anger there in time. The heat *whoomp*ed out of the brick hearth, blowing Macklin's hair forward and his father's hair back, and Macklin didn't even turn to look to see if he'd caught anything else on fire.

His father made a hurried pass with his hand, so he might have, but frankly, Macklin could have burned down the entire compound with his anger.

He'd been *so hurt*. Josue had been the first friend he'd ever had. There were sixteen children total, and the boys hadn't been allowed much contact with the girls. The system was archaic and barbaric, and Macklin had enjoyed being friends with women since he'd left as much as he'd enjoyed being lovers.

But Josue had *meant* something to him, dammit, and Macklin had sent those letters two or three times a year and that card around Yule in the hopes that the young, sensitive boy with the small voice and the biting sense of humor had grown up into a happy man, one who wasn't afraid to speak his mind.

"You're despicable," he hissed, his anger bubbling like molten steel. "You're lucky your power stone hasn't shattered with the force of your deception."

"Macklin," Alistair muttered, backing up. "Be careful. You're... you're dangerously close—"

Macklin could feel it—the poetry, the righteous anger, the pure vindictiveness brought on by hurt. He was going to do it. He was going to cast the ultimate unforgivable spell, a wizard's absolute punishment, the thing that couldn't be taken back. He took a deep breath, the words bubbling on his tongue, and his pocket buzzed, but it wasn't quite enough to stop him.

"May your heart grow—"

His pocket didn't just buzz this time, it rang, and the curse—that inimical, dangerous spell that wished harm upon an enemy and rebounded into the spellcaster's own karma more often than not—stalled in his throat.

He pulled out his phone and saw Jordan's indignant face on the front.

Because that morning, over breakfast, he'd added everybody to his phone, and they'd added him.

Because he was a part of them now. Even if it was for this short-term thing to help get their friends back, he was in their midst.

He hit the green button and held the phone to his ear. "Hey," he said, his voice dropping with tenderness. "How are you doing?"

Jordan was irritated and angry. "I'm at Barty and Alex's, and everybody wants to know if you need us to summon you back."

Macklin laughed, that kind of stomach-loosening laugh that shed all his anger and replaced it with relief. "Wow. Really? Could you do that?"

"Well, yeah! We take notes, Macklin. We're not savages!"

Macklin's spine relaxed. He didn't think that was possible—had, in fact, assumed that such a thing was a matter of words only, but he actually felt it. Every muscle, every sinew attached to his spine and shoulders, went a little noodly, and he could suddenly breathe without anger bubbling in his lungs.

But he'd been using magic enough to keep the power brewing, because he had a feeling he'd need it.

"Give me fifteen minutes," Macklin said. "I should be back by then."

"And if you're not, we can summon you?" Jordan asked. "Is somebody listening?"

"Well, yes. I had to make an unexpected visit to my family," Macklin said, hoping Jordan understood what he was trying to say without saying, and he literally heard Jordan swallow.

"Does he know about us?"

"No, no, don't worry. The old man's all bluster. I told you that."

He heard Jordan's drawn breath and exhaled understanding. "So you haven't told him, but we're still in danger."

"Yeah, maybe half an hour. But seriously, I should be fine."

Another one of those careful breaths. "Good. I'll tell everybody. Anything else I can do?"

And this wasn't code, and it was nothing but the truth. "Tell Bartholomew I would love some cookies when I arrive," Macklin said. Because he'd almost unleashed a curse—a *curse*—upon his father, and only Jordan's timely intervention had stopped him.

"Yeah. I'll do that. We should have dinner ready for you when you get here."

Macklin remembered that moment—Goddess, was it only fifteen minutes ago? They'd been sitting side by side, and he'd felt the heat from Jordan's body seeping through their clothes. Jordan had been looking at him intently, and Macklin had felt like he'd finally met somebody who could see straight into his soul.

Jordan had only eaten a bite of his sandwich, and he was probably starving now. The power he'd held bubbling in his stomach grew a little more active, like a volcano.

Good.

"I'll be there," he said gruffly. "Save me a plate."

"Okay. Take care of yourself, 'kay?"

"Yeah, J." He shortened the name, like Josh did, because he didn't want his father to hear it. But he did want Jordan to know he cared. "I'll do that. See you soon."

"Good."

Jordan rang off, and Macklin pocketed his phone and turned a less angry—and much calmer—face to his father.

"You had no right to do that," he said, voice cold.

"You were a bad influence," his father said, and he sounded… what? Happy? Proud? Like he'd won something?

"And you're a complete asshole. If anybody deserved to be born with powers above ordinary humans, it wouldn't be a soulless, bloodless, Machiavellian piece of shit like you, do you know that?" He wasn't angry enough to hurl an effective curse at the moment, but boy, nothing was going to stop him from making his own observations.

And Alistair's eyes grew wide again—almost limpid. "Macklin, I did not call you here to be insulted like that."

"No? Well then, you *should have called*!" Macklin's voice rose, but it was a controlled yell, so Macklin was reassured. His hands still shook with the nearness of that curse.

"Be that as it may—"

Macklin shook his head. "No, Alistair. There is no 'be that as it may.' That's the entire point. I had a human connection with someone in this house, and you decided to let him think I'd deserted him. For seventeen years. Josue is more than an adult now. He's old enough to make up his mind whether or not to know me. And you hid me from him—hid the fact that I wanted us to be brothers—and until you can make that right, I don't give two shits about what you have to say to me."

With that he swung around his father's study, narrowing his eyes when he saw that the door that usually led to the sitting room of the mansion had "disappeared." It was one of his father's favorite tricks—and one of his most intimidating.

Or it would have been, but by now, Macklin had enough stored power amassed to level his father's study with one sweep of his hand. Fortunately for everybody involved, all Macklin wanted to do was summon a portal back to Jordan.

"Really, Dad?" he asked bitterly. "Do you think I haven't practiced?"

"Really, Macklin?" his father mimicked. "You're going to break the seal of this place to go visit people you barely know?"

"I found out more to like about them in a day than I found to like about *you* in eighteen years," Macklin told him. "And I'll be waiting to hear from Josue to see if any of that has changed."

And with that he held his hand out in front of him and cupped it, summoning the doorway. Then he blew on it until it opened larger, onto his father's carpet.

And then he placed a seal over the portal—and around himself—to keep Alistair from following him or his power signature. It wouldn't work forever, but it might—*might*—keep his father from finding his little coven of friends before Macklin got them all moved away from the neighborhood slipping into hell.

And then he stepped through.

He zipped the portal shut almost immediately after he stepped out, hoping his father got no more than a glimpse of the small cul-de-sac in the late afternoon.

Shit—late afternoon. Almost evening.

As the bright blue glow of the portal faded, Macklin staggered a step or two, drained that suddenly by the power he'd put into teleporting himself from the mansion in the woods in the middle of upstate New York to a suburban neighborhood in California, particularly with all the safeguards he'd used to make sure he wouldn't be followed.

He took another step or two until he came even with his motorcycle, still parked on Jordan's curb, and rested his weight on it until his knees stopped wobbling. As he centered himself, the door to Bartholomew and Alex's house opened and Alex and Simon rushed out, spools of thread and tape in their hands.

"Macklin?" Alex said excitedly, hurrying over to him. "You're back? Good. Jordan was losing his shit. We must have had him repeat what you said about sixty

zillion times, but we've been looking up portals and
tracking spells and you wouldn't believe what else.
Man, you had us really worried."

He moved to the center of the street while he
talked, crouched down near the middle star, and used
the tape and the thread to recreate it. Simon bent at his
side, handing him tape, scissors, thread, much like an
experienced surgery nurse would help a doctor.

"You don't even know me," Macklin said, his
brain a little numb. He'd decided to stand up for this
coven because they were decent people. Because
he'd always believed hedge witches had as much of a
right to practice as the big bad wizards who claimed
superiority. He hadn't expected Jordan's friends to be
as anxious for him as he'd been for them.

"Well, yeah," Alex said, "but you've broken bread,
you've listened to our problems, you're trying to help
us get our friends back—"

"I told you to move," Macklin almost wailed. He'd
hated that moment after breakfast, telling everybody in
the room that this cul-de-sac they'd all tried to make
homey and beautiful and sweet was going to feed off
them and feed off them until they were slaves to the
stucco houses and cracking pavement. That wasn't
what people wanted to hear about their homes.

Alex paused as he was taping stuff down and
glanced at him with a little shrug of c'est la vie. "Well,
yeah, but really all you did was speed up our timeline,
you know? Barty's business was getting too big for our
little house, but Lachlan's got plenty of space for his
extra ovens and refrigerators. In fact, he's got an entire
little house Barty can use for the business, and his sister
was clearing out anyway, so it works fine." He gave
Simon a sideways look. "Simon and I were probably

going to move in together in a couple of months. Whether it works or not, we were heading that way, and I think it's going to work. So I've got a mansion to live in, right? And we've got property for Jordan and Kate and Josh to lease, and even a spot that would be perfect for Cully and Dante, if they want it. Simon's already made calls this afternoon to move portable buildings to the sites, and there should be driveways connecting to the main road by the end of the week. I mean, yeah, we hadn't *planned* on moving, but, you know, we still get to be together, and we might get our friends back. Priorities, man. You helped us find them."

Macklin gave a faint smile, still holding on to the motorcycle.

Wow. Just… wow. He was humbled by this kind of faith—and this kind of optimism. He'd wondered how these people could live here in the presence of this demon for three years and only be feeling it in the last month, but now he knew.

Any group of people who would follow Jordan Bryne had their own magic, their own personal resilience, that would be desperately hard for a demon of apathy to get its teeth into. It had taken a little carelessness, some well-meaning lies, a little self-pity—almost a perfect storm to send their tiny corner of the world spiraling into chaos. But self-pity and too much wine weren't a sin. They all deserved a second chance, and a third, and he'd stand up to his old man again—he'd do it twice; he'd do it once a month for life—to let the people who deserved magic the most keep it in their lives.

A sound distracted him from his wandering thoughts, and he turned to see everybody else stream out of the house, little dog at their heels. Jordan came last, carrying three candles—one black, one red, one white—which he hurried to the center of the star, now outlined in thread and tape and glowing faintly in the lowering gloom.

"Macklin!" he said happily, and Bartholomew took the candles from him without a word, bending down to situate everything while Jordan strode to greet him. "You're here! We were about to try to conjure you back!"

Macklin felt his heart beating in retroactive panic. "Oh, Jordan, you can't do that," he gasped. "My father would find you in a heartbeat and…." He bit his lip, because he wasn't sure if Jordan had told the others what the consequences could be.

"Well, yeah," Jordan said, giving a half smile, "but you weren't taken away of your own free will. We couldn't let you be held somewhere without even trying to get you back." He frowned. "You're looking a little pale. Are you okay?"

Macklin almost held his hand to his heart. Jordan's concern, leveled expressly at *him*, was heady stuff— gorgeous and addicting.

"I summoned a portal myself," Macklin said, still wobbling. "Lots of magic. Need my dinner and a nap now."

Jordan nodded, properly sympathetic, and Macklin felt a bit of rebellion creeping in.

"And a hug," he said, gazing meaningfully at the socially acceptable three feet of space between them.

Jordan gave him a classic eye roll—and a moment's hesitation. Good. He'd been thinking about it.

"J!" Alex said from the ritual circle. And Jordan turned away, saying, "Let me lead the ritual and we'll help you up to Barty's for food and some rest."

Macklin nodded, biting back a sigh. Well, he wasn't defying his father and helping the coven out only to get in Jordan's pants, not that it wouldn't be a perk. He'd just finished telling himself that he really did respect the coven and wanted to keep them safe.

He needed to get used to the idea that Jordan— intense, protective, dedicated Jordan—might not be able to say yes to Macklin when Macklin had asked such a huge thing of Jordan and his friends.

Being there and helping the coven move might have to be enough.

Still, he'd really been hoping for that kiss.

He watched dispiritedly as Jordan took point at the circle, facing west toward the setting sun. He reached out his hands, Bartholomew on his right, Alex on his left, and the circle, Lachlan and Simon included, all joined hands and took a deep, centering breath.

Macklin watched, surprised, as Jordan, using a wizard's oldest and most basic power, lit the candles grouped in the center of the star on the pavement.

The moment the wicks began to flame, the center of the circle began to glow, a vibrant, single-colored wall generated by each individual person there, ranging in color from Simon's clear diamond to Alex's emerald to Barty's amber and Jordan's pure sapphire. Lachlan had a deep blood jasper, Kate's color was amethyst purple, and Josh's was a brilliant aquamarine.

Macklin caught his breath, stunned at the variety and the power formed in the center of a hedge-witches' casting circle, and the sheets of magic joined, became a multifaceted cone, and Jordan started the chant.

New direction, new hope, we have strength to burn brightly.

It was simple—one sentence. But Bartholomew picked it up next, and they repeated it together, and then Lachlan on his right, and so on. When everybody in the circle had taken the chant up, they repeated it two more times for a total of nine, their cone of power burning like a rainbow torch in their midst.

When they were done, they shouted, "So mote it be!" and the cone of power scattered with an almost hypersonic explosion, and Macklin was left breathless, wondering how he hadn't realized what a stunning bunch of witches these people could be.

The wash of magic passed through him, cleansed him, left him feeling revitalized and refreshed, and as he gazed around the neighborhood, he noticed that the film, a foggy gray miasma that seemed to have coated even the air as the day had carried on, was gone, banished by the ritual. Macklin had known how important the ritual was, but he tipped his mental hat again to the scrambling witches who had discovered how to protect their neighborhood and homes.

He took a deep breath, and from very far away he heard Kate and Josh say, "We've got cleanup, Jordan! You get Macklin inside. He's looking a little wobbly."

And then Macklin got the surprise of his life.

He was six feet tall—he knew that. Wiry and fit, he probably weighed in at around 175. He did not expect Jordan Bryne, even at six feet five, to be able to scoop him up, damsel-in-distress style, and carry him across the cul-de-sac and up the walkway to Bartholomew and Alex's house. That didn't stop him from leaning his cheek against Jordan's shoulder and twining his arms around his neck, though. If he was going to be the damsel in distress, he was damned if he didn't get to listen to this man's heartbeat until it came time to be dumped on his ass—or his feet.

Jordan gave a little *oomph* in exertion as he neared the door, and Lachlan rushed to open it for him.

"Well done," he said, sounding as impressed as Macklin was. "I figured Josh could do that—but dude!"

Jordan carried him through the door and deposited him, gently, onto the couch, and Macklin reluctantly let go of his neck.

"I work out," Jordan replied mildly. Then he turned his focus to Macklin. "You hang out here. We'll finish dinner and feed you."

Macklin smiled crookedly. "You still haven't eaten either," he said, voice gruff. "I'm trying to take care of *you*!"

"Well, yeah, but you did super splendiferous wizard things. We just lit a few candles and said some words." Jordan shrugged, and Macklin opened his mouth to protest. Goddess, *that* was the kind of self-deprecation that had gotten them into this situation in the first place. But Jordan had turned to work in the kitchen, and Macklin was left on the couch, sighing.

To his surprise, they didn't eat at the table that night. Instead, Alex brought a plate of food to him about twenty minutes later, saying, "I hope you're not allergic to anything."

Macklin surveyed the plate, which held lots of high-carb comfort things—sausage gravy and potatoes, tender cuts of turkey, and a tossed green salad.

"The sausage is vegan," Alex said, "although the potatoes are made with butter and cheese. We could make you some without if you like."

Macklin shook his head. "Looks wonderful," he said, touched. Good people. He had to remember that. Good. People.

"Macklin, what would you like to drink?" Jordan asked from the kitchen.

Macklin fought off the temptation to say, "A beer," because that would put him right to sleep in this state. "Soda? Coffee?"

"Coffee," Jordan decided for him. "I know how you like it."

As they spoke, the living room began to fill with people, some balancing their plates on their laps, some sitting on the floor by the coffee table, and two of them using TV trays with purple stars strewn across the top, including Macklin, because Bartholomew put one of those in front of him as he gazed bemusedly around.

Jordan came and set a mug of coffee on his tray and then disappeared and returned to sit at his feet in front of the coffee table, a soda on a coaster next to his plate.

"Jordan?" Bartholomew murmured.

"Sure." He glanced apologetically at Macklin. "We're not fanatics. We don't usually say grace, but, you know, it's been a day."

Macklin let out a dry chuckle. "On top of a week on top of a month. I get it."

Jordan bowed his head and murmured, "Merciful Goddess, holy God, unpredictable other, thank you all for letting us get through another one, and thanks for giving Macklin back to us. He's staying to help us out of pure kindness, and we appreciate that. May we all have the strength to rise to the challenges ahead. So may it be."

"So may it be," they all echoed, and Macklin felt a strong, warm, peaceful wind sweeping through his chest, energizing him in a way and making the comfort food in front of him fuel for planning instead of an excuse for an early bedtime.

Talk during dinner was a lot of wrap-up. Jordan and Josh relived the potato bug eruption, and Jordan turned to Macklin with a grimace. "We still haven't checked out the garden—it's probably a disaster."

"Don't look tonight," Lachlan advised, sitting in one of the stuffed chairs with Bartholomew at his feet, eating at the coffee table. "Jordan, it's bad enough you have to go into that house. I'm glad you'll have someone with you this time."

Jordan snorted. "Goddess knows what the song's going to be tonight."

There were generalized groans, and suddenly everybody was belting out their favorite "house tune" from their nights in the witch's cottage. When the whole house joined in for a round of "Bus Stop," Macklin found himself singing along, and they all laughed as the song wound down.

Everybody seemed to take a breath then, and Jordan said, "So. We're really moving, aren't we?"

Macklin took a read of the people who were all sitting, eyes on Jordan.

"Anything to get Dante and Cully out," Bartholomew said.

"We can't go on like this," Alex said, and Josh and Kate nodded along with him.

"I've got property to spare," Simon said, bobbing his chin at Lachlan.

Lachlan, who would be sharing the housing responsibilities, nodded back. "We figure we'll be on trailer rental and hookup, and if you all like the setup and want to build there, you can buy Simon out for your share of the property when this is settled."

"If you want to stay, of course," Simon added.

They all breathed in and out carefully, and Jordan tilted his head back. "I'm really going to hate seeing this neighborhood go," he said rustily, "but I'm already on leave, and now's the time to do it."

"I could quit my job entirely," Kate said, surprising everybody. She shrugged. "You all know it wasn't really my thing. I mean, the dress code alone! But hey, Barty's going to have a full-fledged kitchen and business residence. I can drive a short bumpy country road to his business residence, and we can see how to distribute our goods on a wider scale. I mean—" She looked around at everyone. "—if we're committing to this thing, let's commit. Alex has been doing the taxes, but I can start working the business side of things for all of us and free up Bartholomew to bake."

Bartholomew opened his mouth and shut it. "I… I…." He glanced at Lachlan. "The business pays for itself right now," he said hesitantly. "If, uhm, Lachlan, I could pay your father rent—"

"I don't pay rent—why would you need to?" Lachlan said dryly. "No. You quit your dreaded day job, Bartholomew, and you and Kate make a go of it. Kate—"

"I could do your end too," she said quickly. "We could rent a kiosk somewhere permanent every weekend and sell everybody's goods from there." She smiled hopefully. "You know, lemons to lemonade. We could make it work."

"Let Alex and me run the numbers," Simon told them. "That's what we're good at. We can see how much capital you'll need, and my partners and I can underwrite business loans." He winked at Alex. "You're good for it."

Alex's ruddy complexion was not great at hiding blushes, and Macklin was once again charmed.

"I'm already taking time off work too," Josh said. "Me and J can be your pack mules, renting U-Hauls and moving all the shit into all the trailers and stuff."

"And Macklin and I can spend the evenings figuring out what to do about Dante and Cully," Jordan said. "Because the spell we cast on Samhain is going to have to be very powerful and very private, and we're going to have to create a portal out of nowhere and pull Dante and Cully through. Not just pull them through space but—" He glanced at Macklin, who nodded for him to go on. "—sync them in time. I don't know about you guys, but my memories of them are still split. I've got Dante and Cully together memories and Dante and Cully as roommates memories. That schism is something that needs to be fixed."

"And maybe by Dante and Cully themselves," Macklin said, thinking about the stone on his father's map. Macklin had made that stone change and nobody else.

Jordan looked at him, his severe features made even more stark by exhaustion. "We should talk to them," he said. "Tomorrow. Tell them what's happening to them. See what they can do on their own."

Macklin nodded, his visit with his father still raw. "We need to give them as much agency as we can," he said. "Trying to control their lives will only cripple their ability to help themselves."

Jordan's eyes widened a little. "Experience?" he asked, voice low.

"Later," Macklin said softly, not wanting to share all of the visit right now. But they needed to know some of it. "And because Jordan hasn't told you—because we didn't have a lot of time to discuss it—I need to tell you about why I disappeared."

"Sure," Josh said. "But can we, like, go back for seconds or break to pee first? I feel like that was the first half of a game or something. If shit's about to get real, I need more fuckin' gravy."

Macklin grinned at him. "Absolutely. I feel like I could use a trip to the bathroom myself."

Deliberately, he used Jordan's shoulder to stand up and take his plate to the sink, thanking everyone for their part in the truly sustaining meal as he went.

He half hoped to hear Jordan's knock on the door while he was using the facilities and then washing his hands and face, but alas he was disappointed.

Finally he made his way back to the living room and ensconced himself in his corner of the couch. Jordan gave him a reassuring pat on the foot, and he could put it off no longer.

It was time to tell the truth.

I Want to Hold Your Hand

JORDAN watched Macklin return to the living room and let out a slow breath. God, he looked good.

He'd been pale and wobbly when they'd first seen him outside in the street, but some warmth, some camaraderie, some food had gone a long way. Jordan's people had stepped up, taken Macklin into their midst, and taken his words and advice into their hearts.

He was so relieved.

Watching Macklin disappear had been one of the worst moments of his life—and that included his mother threatening to leave without even saying goodbye. It included the months beforehand, when she was slipping into the abyss and he'd had to wait for his father to get home to eat and lie about skipping school.

It included the short time after Sebastian had left to go study for his second doctorate.

It included the chicken pox, which he'd had at the same time as his father, before Sebastian had returned and taken care of them both.

But Jordan had learned a couple of things from those painful moments. He'd learned that if people were meant to be in your life, they would eventually return. And he'd learned that crying, sobbing, and rending your hair didn't work. Being calm and learning how to re-form your own life around a person's absence was really the only thing that did.

But gah! It had been hard. So much harder than it should have been, given how short a time they'd known each other. But Macklin, from the very first, from his blustery entrance to his subsequent kind, reasonable efforts to help Jordan's friends, had captured him.

It didn't hurt that he was handsome as—quite literally—sin. Jordan had seen marble statues of Lucifer that weren't as appealing as Macklin, with his black hair and blue eyes, his strong jaw and full mouth, and a body that was the epitome of the rangy cowboy with slim hips and surprisingly broad shoulders. But Jordan had seen lots of handsome men and beautiful women, and until now they'd never been his type.

Macklin's good looks weren't part of his ego. Apparently adept use of magic was, but there was more to it than that. Goddess, Jordan just really wanted to know the guy better, and there they'd been, about to—

Do what, Jordan? Kiss? Bare souls? What were you going to do?

Well, whatever it had been, it had been cut rudely short when Macklin blinked out of sight like a faulty hologram.

And Jordan had missed him—acutely, painfully, with a suddenness and panic that had taken his breath away.

He'd hated that. He *hated* that feeling, because Goddess knows he recognized it all over again. Hearing Mack's voice on the other end of the phone had made his knees weak. Barty and Alex had damned near had to catch him, and that was embarrassing.

So watching him walk back into the living room and settle down again on the couch filled Jordan with a heady kind of relief, and some of his control, of the guardedness he was notorious for, slid down Jordan's spine and puddled very, very gently into a pile of smoke.

And then Macklin started to speak.

"When I came storming in here," he said, "and said I was the third wizard son of a third wizard son, I wasn't kidding. Where I come from, that holds a sort of power—but there's a big price for it. Wizards are, well—" He looked around apologetically. "—sort of elitist scum, really. That's why you haven't heard of them. They hole up in compounds in rural parts of the world, have big mansions because somebody in the family is usually a fucking alchemist and is turning plain rocks into gold, platinum, and diamonds as his day job, and they breed. Like bunnies. Pedigreed championship bunnies, with prizes for the best baby bunnies and absolute control over the breeders."

He must have heard Jordan's sucked-in breath, because his hand on Jordan's shoulder was reassuring.

"My father was no different. My mother was his first wife, her family traditionally bore sons, and I was the third. Lucky me. I won the lottery." He gave a snort and shook his head. "Boy, was I a disappointment."

Simon spoke into the pause. "I'm a disappointment too," he said mildly. "I was supposed to be a politician and a diplomat, but I was too damned awkward." He reached across the coffee table to shake Macklin's hand, and Jordan shifted to the side so they could manage. "Congratulations to another disappointment."

Macklin's low chuckle warmed Jordan's stomach. "It's always a pleasure," he said, releasing Simon's hand, and then his voice dropped. "And thank you. All of you. Once I calmed down and stopped ranting, you were all so kind to me—and so desperate. And I...." His gaze slid to Jordan's then, and he gave a little smile. "I was really grateful. I left home at eighteen because I.... Let's just say it was every bit as bad as it sounds. We weren't encouraged to be kind or to be a family. The children were driven to compete against each other, constantly, in academics and athletics and magic. It didn't make for a warm environment. I got out. I went to college, had some relationships, and started a business." He paused for a moment and grimaced.

"What?" Jordan asked quietly.

"I need to remember to tell Billy that I'm going to be gone for a while. We're between big projects, so it shouldn't be a problem, but...." He rolled his eyes. "Housekeeping," he said on a shake of his head. "Anyway, your little family here? Your kindness, your working together and worry for one another? This isn't something I've seen a lot of, and you welcomed me without so much as a blink when I'd been sort of shitty to you, and, you know, thank you."

"Our pleasure," Josh said amiably. "What's the big bad?"

Macklin's faint smile disappeared. "The big bad is that if 'real' wizards find out about the demon in the cul-de-sac, they'll probably strip your coven of its powers and *then* banish the demon, because they're dicks like that, and they wouldn't sit and listen to the fact that the demon wasn't your fault and how your efforts to contain it have been super heroic and really smart. They'll just step in, be dicks, and leave."

The dismayed gasps around the room twisted Jordan's heart. Goddess, they all loved this part of their lives so very much.

"Did you…?" Jordan couldn't even make himself finish the question, and his relief when Macklin shook his head could not be measured in words.

"Didn't tell them a thing," he said, and again he gave one of those reassuring squeezes of Jordan's shoulder. "But the reason my father yanked me through a portal with no goddamned warning was that he knew I was keeping a secret. He doesn't know what it was, and I'm pretty sure I kept him from following me, but that spell we use to pull your friends out of limbo and banish the presence here in the cul-de-sac has got to be… nuclear. I don't want anyone to be able to trace what happens here to a coven of recently relocated witches in the middle of a rural area. Do we all understand?"

Everybody nodded obediently—even Jordan, which didn't come easily to him, and all his friends knew it.

"We'll start working on the spell tonight," Jordan said, and then his shoulders slumped. "But I really do need to see the backyard tomorrow. If there's no sandbox for the Nine, life's going to be really unpleasant for the next week or so."

"Jordan," Bartholomew asked, worried, "what are you going to do with the Nine when we leave?"

Jordan was ready for this one. "Well, I was going to offer them a chance to come live out in Jackson. I mean, they seem to be their own kitty coven. I figured, you know, explain it to them and open my car door and see what happens."

Macklin let out a little laugh.

"What?" Jordan asked.

"Only this coven, and only you, would make that a reasonable option."

Jordan frowned at him, and Macklin smiled gently into his eyes.

"It's a good thing," Macklin said, and Jordan glanced away.

But he was pleased.

"They feel very… personal," he said, and Josh, bless him, was right on board.

"That big gray one is bad*ass*," he said enthusiastically. "But I love the little calico too. I wonder if she'd sleep on our porch, right?"

Jordan chuckled a little and hoped so, and then Macklin pulled them back into the conversation.

"What I'm saying," he insisted, catching everyone's eyes with his own, "is that everybody needs to be very careful working magic in the next week." He gave a stricken Bartholomew a gentle look. "Bartholomew, you're fine. Your magic is hugely powerful but very subtle… and unexpected. Small cantrips—things to find your housekeys or to help you remember to get dinner out of the oven— those are a hedge witch's stock-in-trade. And I think your morning and evening rituals are so woven into the elements—sunrise and sunset—that the power of the times alone can mask them." He glanced around again. "But no more lie-detecting tables or marriage pendants—"

Lachlan and Bartholomew were surprised, and Jordan rolled his eyes.

"I told you," he said dryly.

"And I told Tolly that was fine," Lachlan said firmly. Bartholomew just blushed and fingered the pendant—platinum now, with a raised pentacle charm set over an inscribed gold medallion with runes on either side. The pendants had started out with simple wood, pewter, and colored ribbon. Barty and Lachlan had made one for everybody, although theirs had been special, particularly to them.

Bartholomew had cast a spell of protection over them, and their quality—and power—had grown from there. Barty's and Lachlan's were the most impressive; Jordan was pretty sure he'd seen diamonds winking from Lachlan's medallion, which simply meant the two of them loved with a purity rarely found in mortals, but everybody's medallion had become more and more ornate and powerful as they'd stretched their abilities in their attempts to pull Dante and Cully back into time and place. At present, Jordan's was pure silver, a nine-pointed star instead of the five it had started out with, with a jewel at every point.

Jordan had noticed a distinct similarity between the way his friends aligned themselves when holding hands for the ritual and the colors of the tiny jewels in their place on the star.

The lapis lazuli had appeared in the mirror as he'd been washing his face after Macklin had disappeared.

Go figure.

"Anything else?" Jordan asked.

"Only what we've said." Macklin dropped that comforting hand to his shoulder again, and Jordan couldn't object. "You and I should be working on the big spell together, but we should do most of the work in the witch's cottage. The presence there will mask almost everything we do."

"But won't it know we're trying to kill it?" Simon asked.

Macklin sucked air in through his teeth. "Are we, though? We're trying to *escape* it, and while it reacts to energy we put out, it's not sentient. It can't reason. Escape isn't the same thing as kill. It doesn't 'know' that it will die when we're gone. So we need to keep that word in mind—escape."

"And that's it?" Alex asked.

"Like we said, Jordan and I *really* need to talk to Dante and Cully and tell them what's going on. That's priority one. This isn't going to work without at least some awareness from their side."

Jordan let out a breath. "Yeah. Tomorrow."

"Okay," Macklin said, and tightened that grip on Jordan's shoulder. A silence fell over the room, and the day—another long, awful day—fell on top of Jordan like bricks.

"Bed," Josh said, standing up abruptly. "You guys go to bed. We'll go to bed. Alex and Barty will figure out where *they're* sleeping, and they'll go to bed with their significant others. No, Jordan, don't tell us what to do or how to handle our mornings. We love you, man, but we'll discuss it *tomorrow*. You two look wrecked. Just... wrecked. Stumble back to the center of the demon village and get as much sleep as you can. You'll be out of that dump in, what? Nine days? Eight days? Whatever. On November first, one way or another, you can sleep the sleep of the de— uhm, just."

Kate eyed him sharply. "You were going to say d—"

"*Just!*" Barty and Alex said desperately.

Lachlan finished, "He was going to say *just*, and we're going to leave it there!"

"See?" Josh said, pointing to his chest. "I escaped potato bugs and rabid birds to come reassure my bride. I get some fuckin' respect!"

Kate's panicked expression softened. "You did run across the cul-de-sac shirtless with an umbrella. Fine. You were going to say 'just.'"

Josh grinned happily. "I'm gonna get laid tonight," he promised, and they all laughed.

Jordan stood and offered Macklin a hand up. "Going to make it across the street?" he asked quietly.

"I'm fine," Macklin told him. "I'll sleep really well tonight—three portals in two days!—but I can make it to the cottage."

"Good."

They stepped out into the frosty night, leaving the others to do exactly what they'd said—live their lives as best they could—and Jordan took a drink of cold air scented with woodsmoke.

"Mm." He held his face to the pinpoint stars and sighed happily. "I love this time of year," he said. "Particularly here. We don't get snow, but you can still feel the seasons change. I mean, I wish people wouldn't burn logs, because it's bad for the environment, but it does remind you what time of year it is."

"Yeah," Macklin said. "It gets fucking *cold* in Carson City, but I do love just enough snow on the ground to make winter real."

"Carson City," Jordan said curiously. "Why there?"

Macklin grunted. "Because wizards tend to like densely wooded areas," he said. "Or at least *my* parents did. I figured the desert would be the epitome of hiding in plain sight."

Jordan laughed softly. "It worked?"

"I thought so." Macklin let out a sigh and then groaned. "Augh! My body hurts. Please tell me you have ibuprofen and I don't have to drink infused tea or something."

"I have both." Jordan chuckled. "And some basic healing cantrips. Don't worry—if we can get there before the place lights itself on fire, I can get your muscles to relax."

Macklin let out a groan. "Kid, you have no idea what I'd like you to do to me to get my muscles to relax, but of all nights, tonight I can't *move*!"

Jordan let out a huff of exasperation. "Why?" he demanded. "Why? From almost the first moment you walked into Barty's to the... thing that happened this morning in the bathroom. Why *me*? I don't know if you noticed, but you were *surrounded* by gay men— and one very pretty woman in there, and don't tell me you're not at least bi—but no. You don't flirt with any of *them*. It's me!"

"They're all taken," Macklin said, and Jordan's eyes narrowed as they walked up the crooked paving stones, past the Nine, who seemed to be eyeing them with some exasperation, as if asking what Jordan was up to *now*.

"Great. So you're coming after me because I'm the loser who started this whole—*hey*!"

Macklin had smacked him upside the head. Like a child. Seriously?

"*Abnegation*, Jordan! Holy Hecate, do I really have to point out the dangers of you taking blame that's not yours and shitting on yourself when you're brilliant, gifted, and gorgeous?"

Jordan tripped on the uneven pavement that marked the beginning of the entry alcove. "I'm not shitting on myself," he said, regaining his balance. "I was absolutely candid. This whole thing started when I couldn't get my love life under control!" He whirled to face Macklin under the anemic flickering of the porch light, which, along with every other electric appliance in the neighborhood, seemed to get its jollies with not-so-empty threats. He was very aware that as they stared at each other, the jury of turkeys parked in front of Josh and Kate's house was fast asleep, the starlings were all nesting in the trees around the neighborhood, the crows were all on top of Barty and Alex's house, and the owls—three of them—were lined up on Dante and Cully's. The squirrels slept in their infinity sign, and the snakes had snaked off through the vacant lot across the street that fed into the cul-de-sac.

They were alone.

"You got rejected by stupid people!" Macklin retorted. "Or at least people who could only see the good looks and couldn't see the actual *goodness*. I *have* dated a lot and I *have* had my share. And in my seventeen—yes, *seventeen*—years of freedom since I left the damned wizards' compound that was my childhood home, I have *never* met someone as strong in magic as you are who was also as strong of heart. Nobody I know—not one wizard, not one hedge witch—could have done what you've done, and you keep taking all this terrible responsibility for a mess it took very many fragile, flawed humans to make. It's not fair."

Macklin's voice rose as he spoke impassionedly, and Jordan took a breath and put his fingers against Macklin's lips.

"Hush," he said softly. "That's kind and all, but it doesn't explain why me."

Macklin's mouth curved into a smile under Jordan's fingers. "Because," he said, blowing softly, "you turn me on."

The flush was hard, hot, and immediate, and Macklin's smile went positively gleeful.

"And watching your ears turn purple does *not* make that any less true."

Jordan shook his head and was going to lower his hand to open the door, but then Macklin licked between his two fingers and pulled the middle one into his mouth.

Jordan closed his eyes and fought an uncomfortable burst of arousal. "That's not fair," he murmured.

Macklin let him go with a pop. "But you're getting all het up now, so you do see what I mean, right?"

"I think," Jordan said softly, "that you are the most attractive man I have ever seen. And you are way out of my league." He shoved his hand in his pocket and opened the door.

No candles sat on the fraying area rug to self-light, and no electric lights flickered on or off. It was as though the cottage had exhausted all of its ferocious energy in the potato bug attack that afternoon.

The only thing that reminded him the place was haunted was the Righteous Brothers singing, "You've Lost That Lovin' Feeling," barely loud enough to be heard.

Are You Lonesome Tonight?

"ARE you kidding me?" Macklin asked, face mashed against the couch twenty minutes later. Jordan had warmed him with a bit of healing tea and was now rubbing a concoction of Thieves oil, lavender, and cocoa butter along his bare neck and shoulders.

On the battered plank-wood coffee table sat a mug of tea, a bottle of ibuprofen, and most of Macklin's dignity.

Jordan had let them both in and taken him quickly in hand, fetching the tea, the sweats he'd worn the night before, and a towel, then getting down to business with taking some of the aches and pains of portal travel out of Macklin's joints and muscles.

It was working beautifully, except the cantrip Jordan was reciting was cracking him up.

"You need to close your eyes for a moment 'cause I got this. Let me wash away all your pain with my fingertips" was, of course, being sung to the tune of "You've Lost That Lovin' Feeling."

And the more Macklin bitched, the more verses Jordan added.

"You're trying hard not to show it—"

"Am I?"

But Macklin, I know it! You've lost that portal
    feeling,
Oh, that portal feeling, the aches and the
    pains are healing
Now they're gone, gone, gone, oh-oh-oh....

It was adorable, fun, and working. As Jordan smoothed hard, strong hands down Macklin's spine to his lower back, he could actually feel the pain being pushed out of his muscles.

It was magical.

And it was stopping!

"Baby, baby," he mumbled, "I'll get down on my knees for you, if you would only keep rubbing my back like you wanna do."

Jordan laughed softly and pulled away, wiping his hands on part of the towel sticking out from under Macklin. "Nice try," he said firmly. "But I heard the microwave ding, and I've got one of those ceramic heating pads in there."

"Oh Goddess," Macklin breathed, "you are spoiling me!" Which was great, but Macklin wanted Jordan to be kissing him instead, and he could admit it—he was still peevish about that.

The old leather couch creaked as Jordan stood up, and Macklin missed his heat and the vague sweat of exertion, even in this cold house. Jordan came back and put the heating pad right… there… between Macklin's shoulder blades, and Macklin about melted into the couch.

"There," Jordan said, ruffling his hair, which, as far as Macklin could recall, *nobody* had ever done in his life. "I'm going to step in the shower—I'm still a little smelly from working in the garden—and then do a load of laundry. Is there anything in your jeans you need me to take out?"

"My bike keys and my phone," Macklin told him, barely able to remember. "Jeans are old. Should wash fine."

"Good." Jordan bent to kiss his temple, which surprised Macklin, but not enough to move. "I'll be back in a few to take that off."

"Wait," Macklin said, struggling to wake up. "Wait. You kissed me."

"Sorry," Jordan said mildly. "Moment of weakness."

And then he left, pulling the covers up around Macklin's shoulders and turning the light off as he went. Macklin cursed falling asleep even as he felt it take him over.

EVEN asleep, he sensed the power of the dream, the power of the presence that had slipped in through the cracks of a hedge witch's spell and tried to take over the neighborhood. Abnegation, which on its own wasn't a bad thing but taken to extremes was the death of more talent and promise than Macklin could even fathom, seeped into Macklin's consciousness, but it wasn't attacking Macklin.

Macklin had *forged* himself. His belief in his power was unassailable, and his belief in the man he'd made of the furious teenager who'd run away from home at eighteen and never willingly returned was rock solid.

But Jordan—younger, finding his own way in the magical world and put to the most ferocious of tests that no hedge witch should ever experience, coven leader or not—was full of self-doubt. Oh, not when it counted. Not when his friends were at risk or when they were fully involved in spellwork or strategy. No, Jordan's self-doubt came when he remembered all the things he felt he'd done wrong, all the ways he'd been awkward or demanding or had made well-meaning mistakes.

Jordan's self-doubt was the kind of personal, petty demon that had made mice out of men—or squirrels out of witches—from time immemorial.

And in Macklin's dream, his self-doubt was a jury of turkeys, walking in a sedate circle to the tune of "You've Lost That Lovin' Feeling," stopping every three steps or so to turn and peck at the entrails of a writhing Jordan, who was stretched out in the middle of the cul-de-sac before them.

Macklin thought his own screams were what woke him up, until he rolled off the couch and onto his knees with a thump and heard Jordan screaming through a raw throat.

Macklin barked his shins on the coffee table and wrenched his toes on the doorframe as he stumbled through the living room and into the bedroom. Jordan was sitting up in bed, eyes closed, batting imaginary fiends away from his stomach and chest, and Macklin had to remind himself *not* to work any magic or his father would find them, and that would be worse than this feeble attempt at Jordan's self-esteem.

"Jordan!" he shouted. "Jordan! *J*!"

Jordan stopped screaming and flailing, that long body melting into the mattress in exhaustion and relief.

"Macklin?" he asked, sounding oddly forlorn. "Were there turkeys in here?"

Nice. Ugh, call them demons or presences or pains in the ass, the things that haunted human beings could be cold damned bitches.

"No, baby," Macklin said softly. Without compunction or scruple, he pulled back the fluffy blue comforter and climbed into bed next to him, plumping his pillows before pulling Jordan against his chest. "No turkeys. Just us chickens. No worries."

"Goddess, that dream sucked."

"Yeah, it was a doozy. I dreamed it too. Fuckin' house."

Jordan grunted and the Righteous Brothers wailed away. "I wish we could at least change the tune," he said mournfully. "I used to *like* classic music."

Macklin gave a rusty chuckle, but truth be told, Jordan's lean body next to his was something to be both longed for and feared. He longed for more of this, for Jordan to relax into the bed with him, to take him in lovemaking—all of the good things that could come with two human bodies pressed together. But he really feared making a mistake here. Jordan was so strong, and his heart had been bruised so often by people not nearly as thoughtful as his coven.

So no seduction until Jordan wasn't frightened and worried. Instead, Macklin did what he'd try to do with any friend—he tried to make him laugh.

"You can't hurry *sleep*," he sang. "You'll just have to wait. You see sleep isn't easy, and the turkeys can't decide your fate...."

Jordan chuckled. "That's horrible," he mumbled, already sinking into Macklin's comfort. "Sing the real one, Macklin. Maybe you can't hurry it, but that doesn't mean it's not coming, right?"

Oh! Oh wow. This kid had offered him better than a quick fuck in the dark, hadn't he? Every time Macklin thought he had a handle on Jordan Bryne, Jordan proved he was stronger, smarter, and more luminous than anybody could guess.

"As long as I know it's coming," he whispered. "Jordan Bryne, I could wait an eternity for you."

"Maybe not that long," Jordan said softly. "You smell *really* good."

"You made the body cream," Macklin told him, voice dry.

"Besides that. And your body's all muscly, and you have a great smile...." Jordan fell asleep categorizing all the ways he was attracted to Macklin, and Macklin fell asleep humming "You Can't Hurry Love."

It was almost a spell for happiness right there, wasn't it?

AFTER an ungodly clatter while it was still mostly dark outside, Jordan slipped away for the morning ritual and came back. Macklin felt more than saw him hovering in the doorway, the cool dew of a late October morning still clinging to his aura.

"What'll it hurt," Macklin mumbled, "if you crawl back in bed with me?"

Jordan grunted, and Mack heard the thump of his shoes as he toed them off. His hooded sweatshirt hit the edge of the bed, and then he climbed under the covers, shivering as his body adjusted.

Mack decided to make it easier by draping himself over that lean bit of muscle and pulling him close and tight, because Mack was big into self-sacrifice that way.

Jordan's muffled chuckle warmed the places his skin chilled. "You are shameless."

"You're the best bed partner I've had in a while," Mack told him. Then he snorted and gave the *whole* truth. "The *only* one I've had in a year or so, I guess."

"Why so long?" Jordan asked as some of their shivers died down.

"My business partner got married last year," he said. "Billy's sister and I ended up doing the wedding party sleeping-together thing, and when we woke up together, she was like, 'Look, don't tell my brother. This was a one-night thing, and I don't want to freak him out.' Which, you know, was *my* line. And then it hit me. She's about ten years younger than I am and totally in that place in her life where she's free to wake up with whoever floats her boat. But I'd been doing that sort of thing for ten more years, and it wasn't fun anymore. I mean, *she* was fun, and she's been dating someone long-term, and I'm happy for them, but that drama—will Billy care? Will this freak him out—"

"No and no?" Jordan asked, like it was a foregone conclusion that Mack had confessed.

"Wasn't even surprised," Mack grunted. "And again, fine. I just… it was time. It was time to stop using my shitty childhood as an excuse to fuck everything with knees and not think about the future."

"Mm…," Jordan murmured.

"Mm what?"

"Mm, that's good to know, but—" He yawned, and Mack filled in the blank.

"But we've still got an hour before we need to face the day," Macklin said.

In response, Jordan tightened his arms around Mack's shoulders and pulled him close. Mack buried his face against that amazing chest and breathed in autumn morning, the smell of vanilla-and-lavender candles, and kindness.

And tried not to gloat because Jordan *had* climbed back in bed.

THEY were awakened by a pounding on the door. "Jordan!" Josh called. "J! Man, you gotta stop doin' freaky shit and get out here!"

Jordan's bare feet were on the floor and the thud of his steps through the tiny living room were shaking the house before Macklin even stood up and found his borrowed sweatshirt.

"J!" Josh cried. "Man, your dads are here, and Barty's got cinnamon rolls going, but they already know something's up with the neighborhood, and they apparently had the same freaky-assed dream as everyone else in the cul-de-sac, and Asa's shitting bricks!"

"Fuck!" Jordan cried as he flung the door open, and Mack managed to make it out into the living room in time to catch Josh's arched eyebrow and way-to-go thumbs-up as he did.

Jordan caught the expression, though, and shook his head. "Nothing. Happened."

Josh flicked him in the forehead, and Mack hid a smile behind his hand. "God, you're dumb. But that's a story for another day. Come here and tell your dads there's a demon on their property but that we still love them and want them in our lives."

Jordan groaned and rubbed the back of his neck. "Is there coffee?" he asked.

"And cinnamon rolls. Barty knows how to handle the dads, remember?"

"Why didn't they come here?"

Josh scowled at him. "Because they saw the motorcycle parked outside and thought you might be having a love life. Boy, I'm going to hate to disappoint them about *that*."

"Let me brush my teeth and put on shoes. It's cold," Jordan said, sounding cranky, and Mack had to laugh. Cranky Jordan was sort of fun. Not in control of his temper or his words, he wasn't nasty, merely befuddled and very, very unhappy not to be in control of the situation.

"Sure," Josh said, and then he looked straight at Macklin. "Dude, you disappoint me. That's all I'm saying. You talk the talk, but you gotta get in there and put out for the team." And then he was gone.

"Did you hear that?" Mack taunted as Jordan stalked back toward the bedroom to get to the bathroom. "I'm falling down on the job. I've got to put out for the team!"

Jordan grimaced and tried to brush past him. "Josh means well," he said. "I don't think he realizes how serious this is."

Mack stopped him with hands on his biceps, and while Jordan flexed, he didn't break free when he could have.

"I think he does," Mack said. "Has it occurred to you that he wants to see all his friends settled and happy? Dante and Cully may be the most pressing problem, but I think he believes you're important too."

"I—" Jordan stiffened for a moment, and Mack steeled himself for a fight, and then, to his surprise, Jordan melted a little, thawed. "Of course I want you. Of course I'd love to be having hot sex all night. Do you think I'm stupid?" He moved his hands to Macklin's waist and leaned forward, pressing their foreheads together. "You are all the good things so far, Macklin Quintero. But I need to keep my focus."

Macklin allowed a slow, smug grin to surface. "Sure. Yeah. You keep your focus. But I'll be waiting for when you need a distraction."

Then Jordan rocked his world. He tilted his head and allowed a small smile to twist his lean mouth. "And what part of anything I've said has allowed you to think you'd just be a distraction? If I'm not allowed to self-deprecate, you need to be honest too. You don't want to be my distraction. You want to be my main event. And I want the exact same thing, so maybe we should let things happen apace, okay?"

Macklin swallowed hard. "Oh, kid. You... you are definitely worth waiting for." He grinned, feeling a little evil. "But that's what makes me impatient."

Jordan broke the intimacy by backing off and rolling his eyes. "I'm going to go make myself presentable for *my parents*. If you'd like to do the same, your clothes are in the dryer."

"No," Mack said, feeling smug. "I've got *your*
sweats, *your* flip-flops, *your* spare hooded sweater. I'll
be fine wearing *your* clothes. Declaring my intentions,
as it were."

Jordan sighed. "Whatever. Just declare them fast
or Sebastian is likely to break in."

JORDAN'S fathers were everything Macklin could
have hoped for—and pretty much everything he'd
wished for growing up, no matter which gender they
happened to be.

Asa Bryne was as tall as his son, hale and a little
barrel-chested, but most of that was from work and age.
His waist was still trim, and his blond braid still hung,
thick and only a little traced with gray, down to his
lower back. He had Jordan's cheekbones in a slightly
squarer face and limpid brown eyes.

Sex on a plate—or so Mack thought until he saw
Sebastian.

Shorter than Asa and Jordan but still nearing six
feet, Sebastian had dark curly hair and sky-blue eyes
in an elfin, impish face that still retained its youth even
though Sebastian was probably in his midforties.

Both men were seated at the lie-detector table when
Jordan walked in, and when Jordan sent a fulminating
glance to Alex, Alex merely shrugged.

"They liked the table so much they didn't want to sit
on the couch," he said, meaning infusing every word.

"Fabulous," Jordan said tightly, and Mack
sauntered in after him, feeling very proud of Jordan's
friends.

"So, Big J," Sebastian said, jumping to his feet and
giving Jordan a massive hug, "give us the skinny."

And then, to Mack's surprise, Jordan did exactly that. It was fun to watch, sitting at his elbow, because Mack knew the parts he was leaving out—like jerking Mack himself out of nowhere, asking for help, or casting the spell in the first place because he'd had a bad romantic experience—but other than that, he told them what was important, from the animals to the alarm clocks to the two friends who were trapped in limbo in the house next door.

He told them about magic, which they knew, and about how badly out of hand it was, which they said they'd figured out.

"The squirrels are a dead giveaway," Sebastian said. "Also the cats, the owls, the ravens, the starlings, the motherfucking snakes, and hey, hello, the *dream* your father and I both had last night about turkeys pecking out your insides, which I think will be nightmare fodder for pretty much the rest of our lives."

"You had that too?" Lachlan burst out, and the whole lot of them shivered. "That's creepy."

"Yeah, J," Sebastian agreed. He opened his mouth to say something else, but Asa—who seemed eminently practical—spoke instead.

"What is it you need from us?"

Jordan smiled slightly. "We need you to let us move, all as a group, really quickly. The magic has its own agenda, which we're dealing with, but there's more. Apparently there's a... a presence. A thing that we awakened—"

"It was already here," Macklin broke in, because Jordan needed to stop taking this on his shoulders. "It was sort of built into the witch's cottage, and it took the witch a lot of years to build it up. I don't think even she realized what it was. But it's awake now, and this coven is really strong for hedge witches. So it's been feeding on them, taking away their confidence, their self-esteem—all those things we need to break out of apathy or ennui or even just to advance in our life's journey, this thing is sucking up."

"So it's sort of a battle," Sebastian said thoughtfully. "Between magic, which is movement, and the presence, which is stagnation. They're stuck in the middle." Sebastian gave Jordan an inscrutable look. "Which sort of explains your friends, caught in limbo. They should have been together from the get-go—we could all feel it—but something stuck them, and they didn't make that final connection. So when they got here, abnegation, ennui, apathy—it all sort of worked against them, didn't it?" He glanced around. "It worked against all of you. And why wouldn't it? You were all in that transition part of your life between starting out and reaching for something more. It was a perfect storm."

Jordan nodded. "Yes, exactly. Which is why we need to move. This is a small family neighborhood. All the other houses around this cul-de-sac have kids or grandkids and minivans. The bunch of us, we're ready to move into that sort of setup. Or, you know, the setup at Simon's and Lachlan's, which they're working on for us."

Asa nodded thoughtfully. "Yes, and like I said, we're happy to help you. Just… there's something you're not telling us. Something very… very…."

"Why you?" Sebastian said abruptly.

Jordan dropped his hands from the table and leaned way back, and Mack did too. Abnegation? Self-deprecation? Jordan was the king of it, but that sort of thing needed some heavy-duty lies, especially to oneself, to work.

"Why me what?" he asked.

Everybody else who was seated at the table dropped their hands. Everybody standing took a step back. Glinda, the tiny dog, ran into the other room in a flurry of fur.

Sebastian and Asa gave each other a sideways speaking glance that told of twenty years sharing a bed and sharing lives, and then they both turned toward Jordan.

"Why were you in everybody's turkey nightmare, J?" Sebastian said, as though talking to a child. "I figure Dante and Cully are trapped because they have karmic damage to repair. I'm not going to ask what karmic damage everybody else has—I'm sure they'll tell me while we're moving you all the fuck out of Demon City, here. But your father and I saw our worst fucking nightmare last night—literally—and it revolves around you. So I'm going to ask you, like you're six, why were you the one getting gutted by Thanksgiving dinner?"

"I was the one who initiated the spell," Jordan said, and Asa and Sebastian both sat up as though stung.

"Ouch," Sebastian muttered. "Lachlan, is this thing on a wire or something?"

"No, sir!" Lachlan said, from way back in the kitchen.

Sebastian and Asa both frowned at the same time, not as though stung but as though something had bothered them just enough to annoy. Sebastian put the flat of his hand against the table curiously. Jordan and his friends all shared horrified glances, because the table, obviously, obeyed the spirit of the law and not the letter of it. Anyone *involved* in a conversation that revolved around people sitting at the table had to be honest.

Asa narrowed his brown eyes. "Son," he said mildly, "you and Macklin—have you gotten laid yet?"

"No," Jordan protested. "We're trying to fix shit, Dad! I'm not that irresponsible—that's not fair!"

"Mm." Asa looked at Sebastian, who smiled prettily at Jordan and batted his lashes.

"Do you *want* to hook up with your very sexy rumpled houseguest?" he asked.

Jordan's ears turned purple. "Well, he's hot," he mumbled.

Asa and Sebastian both nodded. "Mm," they said at the same time.

"Bartholomew," Asa said, wincing a little when Bartholomew squeaked from his position at the far corner of the dining room, practically behind the front door.

"Sir?"

"Was this situation Jordan's fault?"

"No, sir," Bartholomew said. "We were supposed to ask for our heart's desire, and we lied because we were afraid of asking for what we really wanted. All of us. So the magic ripped our real wish out of us, and… uhm… we've had to confront that real wish, sort of. I wished for Lachlan, so I had to tell him I was in love with him. You know. That sort of thing."

In that way that some long-term couples have, both of their eyes widened at the exact same moment.

"That sort of thing," Asa said, so casual.

"Yeah, that sort of life-changing thing," Sebastian replied. Then he scowled at Jordan again. "What was your sort of thing, J?"

Macklin's breath caught, and Jordan sent him an agonized look. The question—the big question—that hadn't been answered the day before. And now Jordan had no choice. He had to share his secret with the people he was most embarrassed to show his weakness to, and that included Macklin.

The moment hung long before Jordan closed his eyes, swallowed, and spoke.

"Magic," Jordan said wretchedly, shoulders slumping in defeat. "I... I couldn't seem to find someone, and work... it's brilliant, but it's so sad sometimes. And I loved being in the coven, but I wanted that... that thing in my stomach that lights up whenever we work together. I wanted it in my heart. I wanted *magic*, like you guys when Sebastian and Aunt Bella came to live with us that summer. That was magic!"

Sebastian's eyes grew as vulnerable as a forest animal's, and his lower lip quivered. He shoved his chair back and came over to where Jordan sat, leaned over his stepson's back, and hugged his shoulders. "J, baby. Why would you think you had to reach for that in a spell? Your father and I don't know magic from minnows!"

And Macklin knew, so suddenly, so heartbreakingly, he nearly fell to his knees.

"No," he said softly, remembering those honest words the day before. "No, Jordan. No."

I'm a little autistic, diagnosed, and a little OCD— that's speculation—and moderately ADHD, but I haven't needed medication for it since I hit college. And what all of that equals is that I focus on shit, and I get super intense, and I'm a social nightmare, and that makes people really uncomfortable around me.

Jordan's face twisted, the self-assured coven leader Mack had been falling for so precipitously showing Macklin Quintero the hurt child within.

"Jordan," Mack said, turning in his chair and taking Jordan's hands. "It's not true. None of those… those things you think about yourself, none of those are true!"

Jordan pulled one of his hands away and used it to wipe at angry tears with his palm. Macklin took his hand back and kissed his palm in the center, tasting brine.

"It got hard," Jordan whispered. "Hoping for forever when it was only for a night—or not at all."

"Aw, J," Sebastian murmured, kissing his temple. "You have grown into such an amazing man. I know it's hard to see, because your childhood was rough, but… but—"

Jordan grimaced. "No offense, Sebastian, but you *have* to love me. You're my *dad*!"

Mack *did* go to his knees then, resting his chin on Jordan's thigh and making sure he had Jordan's attention. "Oh, baby, you are so lucky that you think that. Do you think my father loves me? He loves to *control* me, and he's mad that he can't. And that's it. So Sebastian doesn't have to love you, but he does, because you were apparently blessed by the gods in the family department, and don't you forget it."

"I like him," Asa said, standing at Sebastian's side, and Sebastian stood up to give his husband a watery kiss.

"I am aware," Jordan said dryly, and he tried to wipe his face on his shoulder again. Asa thrust a napkin at them, which Mack took and used to mop up Jordan's face.

"And *I* don't have to love you," Macklin said softly. "But give me a few more days—hell, give me a few more hours—and it's very possible I'll find all the reasons in the world why I can't live without you."

It should have been corny. It shouldn't have worked. But besides wanting Jordan in his bed—his lean body, his arctic eyes, that solid intensity that Mack had loved from the beginning—he *wanted* Jordan. The man who could joke about living in a haunted cottage and take a witch's desertion as a way of forging a life he loved.

"Macklin—" Jordan began, but Mack took the hand he held in his own and smacked it on the table, and then put his hand next to it.

"I want you so bad," he said, not caring that Jordan's parents were right there. "And I'm halfway to loving you already. Believe in yourself, J. Believe that you're the kind of person who could send me off a cliff in less than three days, because you are. You're that person—the person I stopped fucking around to find because you don't find the person you want in your life by fucking around."

Under their palms, the table grew warm—a welcome, gentle warmth that Mack took strength from.

"Come on, Jordan," he implored. "Believe in magic. For me."

Jordan looked at their hands on the table and placed his palm up.

Macklin laced their fingers together and pulled their joined hands to his lips, where he kissed Jordan's knuckles.

"Magic," he whispered. "Give us a chance, Jordan Bryne. I'll show you some magic."

And Jordan lowered his head and took Macklin's mouth with his own, a gentle, honest, nothing-held-back kiss, and Macklin took those final steps off the precipice and fell.

And flew.

Dazed and Confused

IF Jordan hadn't been sitting in the middle of Alex and Bartholomew's dining room, surrounded by almost everyone he loved, the kiss would have gone on and on and on and only ended when he and Macklin were sweaty, naked, and sated.

As it was, he was more than a little dazed when he and Mack separated, and he stared at Macklin hungrily, wanting to say so much more.

Unfortunately, the same rules held. Now was not the time.

"So," he said, gulping air and scrubbing his face with his hand. "Now that that's in the air—"

"Oh come on, J!" Kate said, holding her hand to her chest. "That was the most fucking romantic thing

I've ever seen. Let us have a moment to fan ourselves and dream!"

Josh kissed her on the cheek, and she grinned at him, almost shyly.

"Moment over?" Jordan asked, deadpan.

"Fine," she said. "But you know. Romance, people. Don't you ever forget it! But fine. C'mon, J, what next?"

Jordan took a deep breath and searched Macklin's face. Macklin smiled a little and lifted their twined fingers to his lips again. "You're still the leader," he said softly. "You just, you know, got something off your chest."

Jordan would have wished for the ground to open up and swallow him, but in this neighborhood, he knew better.

"I think the same plan as yesterday," he said. "Everybody, the original coven and the dog too, needs to go talk to Dante and Cully," he added after a moment. "They need to hear the truth—and we need to do it as a united front, hand to hand, so they know us and trust us."

He looked at Macklin and sighed. "You need to work on the spell. Most of the books are in the cottage. Some of us will be in to help you later, but you know—"

"Moving everybody in less than a week," Macklin said softly. "I hear you. I'll take whatever help I can get." He grimaced. "I'd really love *your* help, because you are so obviously the power focus, but…."

They both shivered.

"Wait," Asa said. "What was that look? Why did you do that? What's Jordan going to be doing?"

"Nothing, Dad," Jordan said, squeezing his eyes shut. "Just, you know, cleaning the garden and the backyard so the sandbox keeps working for the cats."

"What happened to the backyard?" Sebastian asked.

Jordan covered his eyes with his hands. "It's complicated," he said, and Macklin laughed, resting his head against Jordan's chest since he was still on his knees.

"Dude," Josh said. "It was *epic*. There were *bugs*, and they were *ugly*, and then there were *birds*, and they were *mean*, and then there were *tomatoes*, and they were *self-propelled*!"

"And I think that's what Simon and I will be working on while you talk to Dante and Cully," Lachlan said cheerfully. "Asa? Sebastian? You're more than welcome to join us."

With that, the house cleared out happily, and Jordan stood, helping Macklin to his feet. Jordan watched as Alex and Bartholomew got good-luck kisses and Kate and Josh laced fingers.

He searched Macklin's face for the umpteenth time.

"It's okay, Jordan," Mack said, his eyes fastened on Jordan's face with the same intensity. "I'll give you a good-luck kiss too."

Jordan ducked his head like a middle schooler and bit his lip.

"That would be very nice," he understated, and Macklin answered him with a soft brush of lips on his own. Jordan closed his eyes, savored, and took the comfort because he'd need it, and then they separated and began their day.

"YO!" Dante said happily when they all came streaming into the house. "It's been a long time since we hosted the gang! You guys smell like cinnamon rolls. We'll have to come over next time!" He was a strapping six feet tall, with brown eyes, an Italian nose, and a square, jutting jaw—a young John Travolta or Adrian Zmed.

Bartholomew nodded unhappily and held out a paper bag with two pastries in it. "I brought you some," he said, his eyes darting to the modern black-and-white table in their dining alcove.

The table was empty, but the remains of a pizza still sat on the counter, and Jordan shuddered inwardly. He was pretty sure they were eating and drinking and doing all the human things, but they just happened to walk through walls, and their memories were lost in a temporal void.

Yeah, he agreed with Barty—creepy as fuck.

"Alex!" Cully said as Dante faded out of existence in the living room. "How's it going? You and the accountant still a go?"

"Getting stronger every day," Alex said. "And he's my boss, remember?"

"You little social climber, you." Cully laughed impishly—which suited his doll-like features and pixieish build. He was a good five inches shorter than Dante, but he never looked small when they stood together, because he was always the focus of Dante's attention.

"So," Cully said, disappearing and then reappearing in the blink of an eye, his arms laden with fabrics in all textures and colors, which he dropped on the kitchen table. "What's the occasion? I know we've been a little out of the loop lately—we both seem to be eyeballs deep in projects, you know, but we miss you guys! I can't remember the last time we had a coven meeting. Shouldn't we be preparing for Samhain in a few weeks?"

And that was as good an opening as any. Jordan took the lead, sitting in the battered recliner that was Dante's most beloved possession while everybody else ranged around the room, Alex taking the stuffed chair next to the recliner, and Bartholomew, Kate, and Josh taking the matching tapestry couch. Cully's flair for textures and color was in every nuance of the room, from the magenta lampshades to the turquoise-colored lamps and coffee table. Only the leather recliner stuck out, but it was so much a part of Dante and Cully that even it seemed to deserve its place.

"Guys," Jordan said in his best commanding voice, "I need you both in here at the same time."

Cully blinked and then smiled at Glinda, who was sitting on Alex's lap. "Sure, J. Dante! C'mon, leave your computer and get in here!"

Dante materialized through the tapestry-covered wall that separated the living room from Cully's bedroom, and Cully disappeared, leaving a surprised Glinda who was now staring at empty space.

Jordan scowled. "Dante," he said, standing up, "I need you to take my hand and call Cully in here." He looked at Bartholomew, who read his mind and stood.

"Sure, Jordan," Dante said, sounding bemused. "But you may need to let go of my hand. I mean, you know Cully. He gets jealous."

Jordan nodded, not surprised, but still... surprised. "Okay. Tell Cully to come here and grab Bartholomew's hand. Tell him it's a magic experiment."

He heard Bartholomew's audible swallow and sensed Alex shifting next to him. Kate and Josh had their eyes focused on his face.

"Cully!" Dante called. "Baby, c'mere. Jordan's got a witchy thing he wants us to do. We're all holding hands. Looks sexy!"

Cully's delighted cackle came first.

Then his white-blond hair faded into view.

Then he stood, all of him, from puffy brown trousers, suspenders, and loose-sleeved pirate shirt, which was showy and costumey and just like their friend with the bright blue eyes.

He came into focus, and Bartholomew reached out and took his hand—

And a fierce, cold wind whipped through the house, knocking clothes off the table, pushing down the brightly colored lamps, even upending Dante's old recliner.

Then Dante reached out blindly, searching for Cully's hand in a hurricane, and their hands touched—

—and the wind stopped.

Dante and Cully stared at the faces of everybody in the circle as though seeing them for the first time in a month.

"J...," Dante said roughly, "what in the hell happened?"

Jordan must not have been recovered from his emotional moment with Macklin, because his eyes burned and his throat swelled.

"Oh, guys," he said, voice breaking a little. "You would not believe what we've been going through to get you two back."

The next half hour was a breathless, hurried torrent of storytelling, made harder by the dawning horror on Dante's and Cully's faces as they realized that while they'd had no sense of the passage of time—or the changes made to their memories of the past—the world had been spinning around them. In spite of the wraiths who'd been talking to Jordan and the others when they'd visited, the *real* Dante and Cully had been wandering, lost and untethered to the passage of time. They knew nothing of the changes around them—and they were hurt that those things had taken place without them. Alex and Bartholomew had fallen in love, and Jordan was well on his way. Kate and Josh had abandoned the wedding and were working on a baby instead.

And all of them—all of them—were working their asses off to keep the neighborhood from self-destructing and taking Dante and Cully with it.

Everybody's arms were cramping, their fingers sweating and sliding off each other. Kate and Alex lost their grip on each other's hands at one point, and the wind picked up at monster speed. They managed to clasp hands again, but Jordan was aware that they were on a timetable.

"What do you need us to do?" Dante asked desperately, as it became clear that they couldn't maintain this posture for much longer.

"We all had to confront something," Jordan told him. "We all lied to the magic—all of us. In order to get as far as we have, we all had to confront the lie, confront the person we lied to—even if it was ourself. You guys—you guys need to tell each other your word. The one word you said that night. And you need to face your lies head-on. Because we're moving—

literally, all our possessions *and hell*, and hopefully some high water—to property in Jackson. We have a double-wide and financing for a house and my dads' blessings, guys. We're casting a spell in a week and a half and pulling you out of here. But the only way it will work...."

The wind came up again, whipping at their hair, their clothes, ripping them apart because Dante and Cully may have been stuck in limbo but everyone else had moved on—they weren't supposed to be in this house anymore.

"Is if we take care of our shit," Dante said. He turned toward Cully, who was looking away. "Baby, did you hear me?"

Cully swallowed. "Yeah," he whispered. He gazed up into Jordan's face, and Jordan saw the sadness, the lostness that Cully had worked so hard at masking from the moment Jordan had first met him, at Dante's elbow in the lines for dorm assignments, burdened with brightly flowered luggage and trailing a pink plaid in his wake like a bridal train.

"You can do it, Cully," Jordan said softly, nodding in encouragement. "We will all be here to catch you when it's over. But only if you do the heavy pitching first."

Cully turned to Dante and gave a game smile, and a particularly wicked gust of wind knocked the couch over on its back.

"We'll keep marking the calendar," Jordan shouted. "We love you guys! You can do this!"

And his coven didn't let him down.

"We love you! You can do this," they echoed, and Jordan spoke the words of ending so everybody would let go at the same time.

"So mote it be."

Dante and Cully winked out of sight simultaneously, and all of the furniture that had been upended was magically put to rights.

Jordan wanted to stretch his arms over his head and do some twists to get rid of the cramping, but the temperature in the house had dropped significantly, to the point where they could all see their breath.

"T-t-time t-t-o—"

Jordan didn't wait for Bartholomew to finish the sentence. Instead he turned and headed for the door, using the sleeve of his sweatshirt to open it to keep his hand from sticking to the frosty handle. They all filed out into a world where the long shadows of October had lengthened to evening, and the chilly, humid air was almost balmy compared to the dry ice of the cold in that once-happy living room.

They filed down the pathway, stepped heavily over the squirrels, skirted the jury of turkeys murmuring quietly among themselves—and avoided the turkey crap that they'd been trying to clean up for the past month—and made their way wearily to the center of the cul-de-sac. Jordan sank down, setting his bottom on the sidewalk, not caring who sat with him.

They all sat with him.

"I'm exhausted," he said out of nowhere. "How long were we in there?"

Bartholomew pulled his phone out of his pocket. "Outside time says five hours, but I swear you didn't talk that long."

"We can't afford to go in there again," Jordan said. "Not as a group. One of us, every day, needs to go in and mark the calendar—and we need to make sure someone's standing by the door to show that person the way out." He closed his eyes and breathed in. "You can hear the freeway from here," he said, although it had never occurred to him before. Folsom had a lot of modern suburbs that wound among gentle hills, but they were closer to Highway Fifty than anybody liked to contemplate.

"You can't hear it in Jackson," Bartholomew said. "It's out there, really. It's nice."

Jordan saw a faint smile on Barty's full lips. He was probably thinking about Lachlan, but he was also looking forward to their new home.

"Then we'll follow you," he said. "We'll close our eyes and jump into the breach and do our best. It's all we can do."

Bartholomew's smile gave him heart.

"Guys," Alex said hesitantly, "the, uh, sun's getting close!"

Jordan heaved to his feet and stretched out his hand for Bartholomew, and together they pulled everybody to their feet and made their way to the star in the center of the cul-de-sac.

"What's it gonna be, J?" Josh asked as they clasped hands again.

"Holy Goddess, Merciful God, let us find our way home. So may it be."

"So may it be," they answered, and while the words were simple, and they were tired, the power they'd gotten so adept at raising continued to do its thing, spreading out over their neighborhood and freeing it from the painful things that had crept in during the day.

The sun went down, and Jordan found himself in a flurry of hugs.

"On our own tonight," he said, smiling faintly. "Let's go find where all our people went. Sebastian and Dad are probably in my house. Everyone have a good night. See you in the morning." Their car was still out front, behind Macklin's motorcycle.

Poor Macklin—in the middle of riding his motorcycle and sucked into this disaster. But then.... *Give me a few hours and I'll probably be in love with you.*

Jordan wobbled on his feet, thinking about it.

"Night, J!"

And they dispersed, probably as tired of magic and of strategizing and of worry and of planning the rest of their lives in a heartbeat as he was.

He wandered up his walk, giving the cats a little wave and appreciating their nods of respect back before letting himself into the cottage.

His dads were sitting at the kitchen table while Macklin—who had apparently gone for staples—cooked a frittata at the little stove using ingredients chopped and lined up neatly on the cutting board that fit under the counter.

"Wow, J," Sebastian said as he entered. "You look *beat.* You guys were gone forever. How'd it go?"

Jordan thought about it. "Well," he said, realizing it was true, "I think... I think they're on board." He frowned. "How'd it go for you guys?"

Sebastian's eyes narrowed. "Remember when you were little and we were talking over the computer and you threw up on the camera?"

Jordan grimaced. "Yeah."

"This wasn't worse, but it was close."

Jordan chuckled and draped his arms over his fathers' shoulders, kissing them both on the cheek.

"Thank you," he said softly, "for helping me clean up my mess."

"It's what we're here for," Asa said cheerfully, kissing his temple. "And Simon and Lachlan have your lives planned to the nanosecond over the next week. I think you're in good hands now that we've cleaned up the backyard." His father nodded soberly. "I think you all can pull this off."

Jordan turned to where Macklin stood, wiping his hands on a towel and looking hopefully at him. It took Jordan a moment to realize what he wanted.

And then?

It was the most natural thing in the world to walk up to him, put his hands on Macklin's hips, and kiss him hello.

Mack's lips curved up underneath Jordan's in a happy smile—parting a little so Jordan could taste—and he hummed softly.

Wildfire threatened to sweep through them both, and Jordan pulled back hastily.

Macklin's low chuckle told him he understood. "You're just in time," he said. "Set the table for dinner?"

And like that, some of the exhaustion washed away from him. This man—strong, funny, *fascinating*, and sexy as hell—had cooked him and his parents dinner. Jordan might be moving and Macklin not be there to stay, but right then, in that moment, everything in Jordan's world was right. He set the table, and the conversation turned to the practicalities of moving. Then, as Macklin served them frittata and fried potatoes, it turned to other things.

They talked about Jordan's childhood and Macklin's business. Asa talked about his work in contracting, and Sebastian talked about working in a bookstore and teaching community classes in art history on the side.

It was a pleasant evening, all things considered, and when the dishes had been washed and Jordan's parents hugged him goodbye, he was left feeling not exhausted, but energized.

Excited, even, about the whole new world, the different turn his life had taken, and the man, currently standing at the sink, wiping the last of the dinner off the counter, who was part of it all now.

And suddenly it didn't matter if Macklin dropped his whole life and moved here because Jordan needed him, or if he couldn't. It didn't matter if their future was in the cards, or if it wasn't.

What mattered was that when Jordan had most despaired about himself, this man—*this man*—had held strong to faith, when he had, perhaps, the most tenuous of reasons to believe.

Jordan's entire world had hit the ground with a thump, rearranged itself, and showed him how different reality could look in a matter of days.

"What?" Macklin asked, grinning at him. His dark, curly hair had been pulled back into a stumpy queue while he worked, and Jordan wanted to touch it. His blue eyes—so piercing—seemed especially farsighted this evening, and Jordan remembered what it felt like when those eyes were trained on him—just him—with all the hope in the world.

"Did you really mean it?" Jordan asked. "When you said you could fall in love with me before all this was over?"

He actually saw Macklin's Adam's apple bob. "Yeah," he said gruffly. "Why?"

"Because I fell in love with you right here. Right now. And I want you so badly my chest hurts with it. And I was hoping…."

Macklin's smile illuminated the tiny witch's cottage. "Yes," he whispered. "Yes."

Jordan was on him in two strides, taking Macklin's stubbled cheeks between his palms and plundering that sexy, sinful mouth with his own.

Ain't No Mountain High Enough

MACKLIN thought he'd been prepared—but there was no way he could have been. He'd tasted Jordan, touched him a few brief times, had Jordan's hands on his body the night before, but that had been Jordan holding back, staunching the wildfire assault to Mack's senses, trying to keep things in control.

This was the whirlwind of intensity Mack had always sensed under the surface, the great and terrible need Jordan had been afraid would crush anybody he unleashed it upon.

Mack answered his kiss like a starving man, his hunger feeding the man who fed on him. He couldn't taste enough, devour enough, *get enough* of Jordan Bryne's kisses, of his mouth on Mack's skin, nipping, licking, sucking. His teeth, closing gently on the join of Mack's neck and shoulder, sent arousal staggering through his synapses, and he cried out, his knees going weak. He found himself shoved back against the kitchen counter, and although Jordan kept kissing him, he very deliberately pulled Mack's hands out from under Jordan's own sweatshirt and placed them on the countertop. He pulled back, dragging Mack's lower lip playfully between his teeth as he did, and then focused those blazing arctic eyes on Mack's own.

"Stay," he commanded, and there was no uncertainty in his voice. With a shock Macklin realized that, after seventeen years of living on his own to do what he chose, the thing he chose to do was put his body, put his *pleasure*, in the hands of someone else.

More specifically, the hands of Jordan Bryne.

Jordan stripped Mack's sweatshirt over his head and then grimaced. "Still cold," he murmured but rucked up Macklin's shirt enough to kiss down his throat and suckle a pebbled, sensitive nipple. His hands mapped Macklin's skin, and every time he pulled with his mouth, Mack's chest arched, closer, closer! He wove his fingers through Jordan's hair and held him tight.

Jordan nipped gently and moved his mouth to the other nipple, and Mack had to drop one hand, doing what Jordan had told him to do—stay. Otherwise his knees really would have buckled, and they would have ended up on the kitchen floor, and Mack still wouldn't have cared, but he had the feeling he knew where Jordan was going with this, and he wanted it badly.

Jordan sucked on his nipple again, this time shoving at Mack's jeans, undoing the fly as he went. Mack's jeans and briefs puddled on the floor around his ankles, exposing his cock, and he moaned at the touch of the cool air alone.

But the cool air wasn't the only thing touching him in a moment. Jordan sank to his knees without ceremony, hot mouth open, engulfing him in one smooth stroke. First he laved, his mouth wet and welcoming, then he sucked, pulling back and thrusting forward, teasing with his tongue between strokes.

His hands weren't idle either—one was cupping Macklin's balls, fondling gently, and the other was kneading his backside aggressively, parting him, exposing him to the air, letting him know to be ready for what was to come.

Macklin was hardly prepared for what was happening *now*.

Jordan kept sucking, kept stroking, merciless, demanding, and Macklin tilted his head back and groaned from his stomach, his entire body washing cold, his vision exploding as a fast-and-furious orgasm rioted behind his eyes.

His cock spat hotly, and Jordan swallowed, not missing a stroke with his hard, lean mouth.

Macklin seemed to come forever, finally giving a gasp as his head became too sensitive, and he tugged at Jordan's white-blond hair with the fingers of one hand. Jordan pushed up, crowding Mack's mostly naked body with his own, not even bothering to wipe the come-glaze off his lips, chin, and cheeks.

He was the sexiest goddamned thing Macklin had ever seen.

"Kiss me," he panted, and Jordan's lips became an evil slash of a grin before he reclaimed Macklin's mouth, thrusting his tongue inside and letting Macklin suck the last of the spend from it as Macklin whimpered. He'd come, but he was not sated, and he wanted everything Jordan offered when Jordan ground his denim-covered cock up against Macklin's thigh.

He whimpered, needing more, and Jordan pulled back, eyes wicked.

"You want it?"

"Goddess, yes," Macklin begged. "All of it. Everything. Please."

"Meet me in the bedroom," Jordan whispered in his ear, tugging at his earlobe with his teeth. "Lube and condoms in the drawer."

"I'm negative," Mack panted. "On PrEP."

"Me too," Jordan told him, moving to the other ear. "Do you trust me?"

With his magic, with his body, with his heart, with his *soul*. "With my life," he said, knowing that it was true.

"Then make yourself ready." Jordan tore himself away, leaving Mack to step out of his boots and his pants and ramble, half-naked, body burning in the chill, as Jordan turned off the lights, said blessings at all the doorframes, and, Macklin suspected, left bowls of kibble outside for the Nine, whom Macklin wouldn't want to piss off either.

By the time Jordan came into the bedroom, shedding his sweatshirt and shirt over his head and heading for the bathroom to wash his hands, Macklin had undressed and was lying under the covers, warming the sheets, his fingers slick with lube behind him.

He was teasing himself, sweeping his wet forefinger down his crease, along his pucker, darting in, swirling around.

It was something he'd do alone, when he was in the mood for sex but had no one to help him out, but here, now, with Jordan, he knew it was more than that.

It was preparation.

Jordan wouldn't waste time with foreplay—not tonight. Jordan would take him as mercilessly and thoroughly here as he had in the kitchen.

Macklin wanted nothing less.

Jordan returned to the side of the bed, kicked off his sneakers and started stripping off his jeans and briefs, and Macklin's breath caught, watching him in the lamplight.

"What?" Jordan asked, his innocence real.

"Your body is…." Mack let out a low whistle. It was the body of a man with a long, lean build who could still lift Macklin like a damsel in distress. "Very nice."

Jordan smiled shyly, stumbling a little as he paused to wind the clock and set the alarm, still vigilant even when Mack could see the flush of passion staining his cheeks.

"I'm glad you like," he mumbled, sliding into bed. He hid his shyness by tucking his face against Mack's throat, kissing and licking again. Mack *hmm*ed, and Jordan moved down his stomach, pausing to trace along Mack's ribs with his tongue. "I like too."

Mack gasped and tilted his head back, thrusting his fingers inside and breathing hard. Jordan pulled away from his hip bone and eyed him with amusement.

"You making yourself ready?" he asked, his voice a low purr.

"Yes!" Macklin begged.

Jordan sat up on his knees, and Mack got a look at his erection, long and girthy and weeping for him.

Mack moaned and removed his fingers, wiping them on a tissue he'd left ready even as he pushed himself forward so he could taste the head of Jordan's cock.

"Mm…." Jordan tilted his head back and tangled his fingers in Macklin's hair. "I am going to use your mouth someday until it drips come."

Mack thrust his head down until he could taste Jordan in the back of his throat and swallowed, taking the threat as a promise, and Jordan gratified him with a few short, quick thrusts before he pulled reluctantly away.

"But first," he said gruffly, "you have something ready for me, don't you?"

Macklin splayed his legs and reached down to part his cheeks and expose himself to his new lover.

Jordan hummed and reached down to play with him, testing, one finger, two. Mack groaned and planted his feet, arching his back so Jordan had access. Jordan spread his two fingers and ripped another groan out of Macklin's throat, and right when Macklin was going to beg, Jordan added one more.

"*Ah Goddess, yes!*" Mack's hips arched off the bed, and he tried not to scream, tried not to beg, tried not to gibber.

Tried not to come.

He had to master himself, his whole body shaking, and when he came to, he found that Jordan had shoved a pillow under his hips and was still fingerfucking him while he mouthed the base of Macklin's cock.

And Macklin was his, given over, completely submissive, so happy to need.

"Please," he begged. "I need you inside me. You, Jordan—*you.*"

Jordan's fingers disappeared, and he wanted to cry, because he felt empty. Jordan positioned himself between Mack's spread thighs, and Macklin felt a curious wrenching, a moment in which he freed his soul from the last constraints of who he'd been three days ago and embraced the man taking him now.

Then Jordan was at his entrance, slick and wide, too big to slide inside, too gentle to batter. He thrust, bit by bit, until Mack cried out, sweating. Just when Mack thought he couldn't stand it anymore, a ring of fire behind his eyes as Jordan's cock took over his body completely, Jordan's head popped in, and he gave a sigh of relief.

Of total surrender.

"Good?" Jordan whispered, close—so close— those eyes boring into Macklin's, his lips tender on Mack's forehead.

"Yes," Mack said, "because it's you."

He'd had lovers before, but this was all brand-new. Not just Jordan's size, but the burning, almost under Mack's skin, as Jordan pumped forward and back. Macklin kneaded his chest, his shoulders, cupped his neck, their joining becoming the focus of his being, of the world, of the universe.

With a terrible shudder, he lost control, clutching at Jordan's shoulders without care for whether he grabbed too tight, crying out as his body washed hot and cold again, but this time it was searing fire, and this time it was blazing ice.

"Jordan!" he cried, suddenly afraid, and Jordan's hips began to move faster, his thrusts coming harder, his possession surer and more intimate as Macklin shuddered around him. Macklin's orgasm endured, shaking his body viscerally as Jordan fucked, until a gorgeous, terrible ball of magic built in Macklin's chest, the most terrifying and wonderous thing he'd ever felt as a wizard—and definitely the most terrifying, wonderous thing he'd ever felt as a man.

"Jordan!" he sobbed, wrapping his legs around Jordan's hips. "Augh! Goddess! Now!"

And Jordan cried out in climax as Macklin tilted his head back and screamed.

As Jordan fell against him, hips stuttering in orgasm, Macklin was vaguely aware of a series of small thumps around them, and the garden-and-sulfur smell he'd always associated with wizard's magic.

"Gah!" he managed, Jordan's heavy weight pinning him to the bed so thoroughly he never wanted to get up. "I thought I knew what sex was. Goddess, Jordan...."

"What was that?" Jordan asked, not tensing in the least, his body still a sprawled, limp, satiated burden in Macklin's arms.

Macklin looked sideways and *hmph*ed.

"What?" Jordan asked, but he was busy licking the sweat off Macklin's neck, so he must not have been that excited about the strange sound and the new objects in the room.

"My clothes," Macklin muttered. "My dresser showed up in the corner." A part of him brightened. "I can wear a different pair of jeans tomorrow. And my own sweater."

Jordan growled against his shoulder. "I like you in my clothes."

Well, Macklin couldn't lie. So did he. "My own underwear," he panted, Jordan's tongue on his throat making him want to start the whole thing again.

"No underwear," Jordan mumbled, nibbling on his ear.

"Okay, fine," Macklin conceded, because he'd already admitted to himself and Jordan that Jordan could have his way with anything on Macklin's body. "But I want to suck your cock sometime. I want to taste your come."

Jordan growled and began rocking again inside him, and to Macklin's surprise, he was hard again. "Tomorrow," Jordan told him, pushing up and thrusting some more into Macklin's sloppy, dilated entrance.

Knowing he was used and stretched for and from Jordan's pleasure just made him more sensitive.

"Yeah, fine—God, harder—"

This time, when he screamed, his television parked itself in the front room, leaning against the bookshelves filled with spells.

But they wouldn't see that until the morning, on their way out to the ritual, and by then, Macklin had found time to suck Jordan's cock.

His mouth tasted like come in the morning.

THEY went back to sleep for another two hours, cuddling together in their sweats because the house seemed to have upped the ante on the freezing people to death in its environs. When they woke up, Jordan made them both travel mugs of coffee, and Macklin grabbed a clean pair of jeans from his own drawer and a T-shirt and hooded sweatshirt from Jordan on his way to the shower. He went to get a pair of briefs from his own drawer too, and Jordan gave him an arch look.

"You weren't serious," Mack said, laughing.

Both eyebrows went up. "I wasn't?"

"I don't wax," Mack said with dignity. "My pubes'll get… you know. Ouch."

Jordan rolled his eyes. "Fine." His expression turned intense, though. "But I… I can't guarantee they'll stay on all day. We're going to be doing spellwork in here, and touching in here, and… and…." He moved closer to where Mack stood balancing one hand on the sturdy maple wood of his familiar dresser in this increasingly familiar place. With a gentle hand, Jordan shoved Macklin's hair back from his eyes, fingers tangling in the ends as he tugged gently. "I want you all over again," he said throatily. "I'll want you until you decide to leave me."

Macklin shot him a crooked smile. "J, why do you think all my stuff arrived here via portal after we made love?"

Jordan gave the dresser a sideways glance. "I, uhm, didn't want to ask."

Mack lunged up to take Jordan's mouth, only to find himself pressed back against his dresser, ravaged and wobbly, clutching Jordan's chest. "I… I'd decided to stay," he rasped, knowing it was forward. Not caring. "I felt it in my bones last night when we'd… after we'd…."

Jordan's hands were long-fingered, exacting, tight-sinewed, and they were hard on his biceps and hips as he maneuvered Macklin around, bending him over the couch and stripping his own sweats off Macklin's hips. Macklin did what he'd done the night before: gave himself over, allowed the sudden, brutal arousal to sweep him, make him hard, wash his body with sweat.

Jordan had apparently been carrying lubricant in his sweater pocket, dreaming of this, and Macklin would have laughed, but the slickness of the lube, warmed by Jordan's body, made him gasp instead. And then Jordan was inside him again. He was sensitive—a little sore, even—but this was possession in its most basic form. As he rushed to his climax, his body already wrung out by their passionate night, his vision went white with the pleasure/pain of being given completely to somebody else.

Someone he loved.

Jordan.

He cried out, a few drops of spend scalding the end of his cockhead, because that's all he had left. Jordan buried his face against Macklin's neck and howled, wrapped his arms around Macklin's chest, and held him tight as he finished his own climax, his cock still thrusting weakly in aftermath.

Jordan's shoulders shook for a moment, and he whispered harshly in Macklin's ear.

"I've never had somebody mine before. Dante and Cully, they were perfect from the moment they met, and they denied it and denied it and denied it until their home is a vortex of wrongness. I won't do that with you. Move in. Be mine. Stay with me. As long as you can stand me. I'll love you. I love you now. I'll love you long after you go. But we'll be together, and we'll be right, and that's all I can do, all I can learn from this." Jordan's shoulders convulsed around his back. Macklin felt the wetness of Jordan's cheeks against the back of his neck. "If I can be enough for you, maybe this is the lesson I needed to learn."

Macklin shuddered, a hint of premonition creeping over him at the worst time. "I love you. We made magic last night, and the magic decided I should be here, with you. It moves quicker than people do, but I'm not stupid. I know where I belong."

Jordan laughed softly, brokenly, his arms tightening. Macklin couldn't breathe, but he didn't care.

Then his body jerked, and the front pocket of his jeans buzzed against the back of Macklin's thigh. They both pulled away, and Macklin showered and dressed quickly, shivering in the cold house. When he emerged, Jordan had combed his hair and rinsed himself off in the bathroom sink, and all there was left to do was grab their coffees and go.

IF Macklin had been expecting a round of applause or hooting and hollering or frat-house bullshit when he and Jordan walked in together, he was sorely disappointed. But as he sat at the table and looked around at the sober Alex, the shy Bartholomew, the sweetly earnest Kate and Josh, he realized that these were not the people who would do that—not when they didn't know Macklin that well.

It warmed him, in a way.

They sat down and planned as usual, Jordan taking point—and listening to reports from Alex and Bartholomew since Simon and Lachlan were out and about. He heard questions and made suggestions and then generally let everyone else tell him their plans. Macklin could see this was how they'd interacted since college, with Jordan running the show but hearing everybody else's input, and he wondered if they'd realized that they were training themselves for something as intense as fixing a botched spell in a surprisingly powerful hedge-witches' coven.

And then Jordan said something that called Macklin's attention back to the proceedings.

"Okay, we're going to need the stuff in the witch's cottage there until the last day. As in, we get up in the morning, do the ritual, throw everything in the moving van and then throw it in the trailer, and get back here in time for sunset ritual. Everybody else can be moved out before then—including Dante and Cully. I think if we go in two at a time to take out their big furniture, it might keep them grounded. Leave the beds till last, but move the rest of their house first if you have to. I think that will work."

Macklin elbowed him and said, "All I need of my stuff is a duffel of clothes. Everything else can go tomorrow."

Jordan nodded. "Well, the day after is the soonest we can get a moving van, so we've got two days to pack up and plan." He grimaced. "You know, we all live pretty simply. I... it would be nice if this works out. If we can buy property from Simon, have my dad design a house that can accumulate some stuff. Have a study *and* a living room *and* a guest room." He flashed them all a grin. "You know. Like a grown-up!"

Everybody laughed a little, but it was Alex who noticed the new thing.

"Hey, speaking of moving Macklin's stuff, how is it he *has* any? I noticed an SUV parked on the curb in front of Jordan's—is that yours too?"

Macklin nodded, his face heating. Nobody had said anything about it at the sunrise ritual, but they were all so tired that getting out there and raising power was an accomplishment.

"I, uh... well, there was a power surge last night, and all my stuff appeared via portal," he said, because he was sitting at the lie-detector table and that was how you did things if you didn't want to say, "Jordan fucked me silly and I committed my life to him even though I am supposedly a grown-assed man."

But judging by the way everybody's eyebrows rose, he figured it was something he didn't have to say.

"A power surge," Kate repeated carefully.

"Well, yeah. After Jordan and I, uhm, went to bed."

Kate let out a healthy laugh. "Jordan?" she said, tilting her head at him, and Macklin figured that, for as long as he lived, he would never get tired of those crescents of flush painting Jordan's knife-blade cheekbones.

"We did some things," Jordan said, rolling his eyes at his own "niceness." "We did some grown-up things, and they were important to us. And apparently the magic figured Macklin should stay, because it shipped all the stuff he'll need into the house. By the way, I now have his big-assed TV to put in my living room, so guess who's on for movie night?"

"Dude," Josh said, looking at Macklin in wonder. "Your *car*?"

Macklin shrugged. "It was a, uhm, really big power surge."

And that, of all things, tipped the scale. Everybody laughed happily, and Macklin was being congratulated and deluged in good wishes. Not tacky hoots and hollers—hugs and welcomes to the coven. All those years he'd spent being a wizard unto himself, hating magic and his birthright because it had only ever come with loneliness and pain, and here he was, in the center of a hedge-witches' coven, being welcomed like family.

His chest swelled, and his eyes burned, and a scarf he'd bought at a craft fair, which had lurked in the back of his closet because it was too nice to wear, dropped from the ceiling and onto the kitchen table.

All of the babbling ceased, and Macklin smiled as he took the hint and wrapped the scarf around Jordan's neck, tucking it in to keep him warm.

"Thank you, guys," he said as he leaned over to kiss Jordan's cheek. "I... I apparently haven't felt like I was home in a very long time."

He felt it then—a foreboding, the niggling that something was wrong. But they had less than nine days to rearrange everybody's life. Foreboding or not, all of them were hurtling to the future, and Macklin had no choice—and no desire—to fear what remained of the past.

Bad Moon Rising

MACKLIN lay sprawled beneath him, one arm flung over his eyes, bare chest sheened with sweat as Jordan shuddered above him, pouring his seed and his soul into Macklin's amazing body. Macklin's spend cooled on both their stomachs from his climax, and everything about his posture—wildly curling hair, the sweat dripping on his throat, the way he sobbed for breath— indicated complete surrender.

It was that last thought that sent Jordan over, squeezing his eyes shut at the last moment as climax overtook him, everything from his cock to his taint to his balls wringing itself tightly into knots before the ultimate release.

In the wash of white behind his eyes after orgasm took him, he saw....

A room. A dark-wooded room, with carefully beige carpets, tapestries on the wall, and a great board on a heavy teak desk with rocks of various sizes and colors on it.

One of the stones was glowing with Jordan's sapphire blue and was shot through with gold like lapis lazuli, except… both.

Them. Jordan and Macklin.

Jordan sucked in a breath, pulled himself back from the room, and collapsed on top of Macklin, shaking with aftermath.

And a little with fear.

"Jordan?" Mack's hands in his hair, cupping his neck, skating his shoulders, were so very welcome. They pulled him farther into his bedroom, practically stripped down now with their move so close, only a knapsack of clothes for the two of them on the floor at the foot of the bed.

Two nights, two days. That's all they had. After a week filled with furious, nonstop activity, it all came down to everybody moving their bed frames tomorrow in a couple of rented U-Hauls and sleeping on their mattresses tomorrow night, the majority of the heavy furniture and their clothes already moved and unpacked, along with their dishes, including most of Bartholomew's bakeware.

He'd kept some of it, though, and a single refrigerator so they could still meet at his and Alex's house for one meal a day—to plan, to vent, to spitball questions, generally to gather after the morning ritual and get their shit together.

Bartholomew couldn't make them cinnamon rolls without at least one mixer, some bowls, and his favorite pans. And the last forlorn stove, since most of his hard-core catering equipment had already been dismantled and moved to its new location on Lachlan's property.

Macklin had called his business partner, which still made Jordan catch his breath. He'd been there for the conversation, Macklin talking genially to a guy named Billy, giving Billy the rights to the business they'd started from scratch, as long as Billy would refer all of the clients in Macklin's general area. They'd split amicably, and Macklin had even called a real estate agent and movers, planning to drive to Carson City and make the move official after they got Dante and Cully back.

Jordan had started the ball rolling to transfer from the crime lab in Sacramento to the one in Amador County, because it was closer. But none of this had anything to do with what he'd just seen as they'd been making love.

"Mack?" Jordan asked, sounding lost. He blinked hard and harder and still couldn't shake the vision of the room with the giant black marble fireplace and the tapestries on the walls.

And no door.

"Do you know a room without a door?" he asked. He'd come inside Macklin, and he was still a little hard, but he remembered that stone—sapphire blue and lapis lazuli—and he didn't want to move. When they were together like this, inside each other, nobody would know that stone was the two of them.

They were protected together.

"A what?"

The panic in Mack's voice was enough to call Jordan back to himself, to the witch's cottage, to their second-to-last night in the cottage before the final move—and the final spell—on the five hilltops on Simon's property during the Samhain bonfire.

"A room with no door," Jordan said, very specifically. "A big black fireplace, and a… it was like a chessboard, but it was a map instead, and there were… rocks. Crystals. Strewn all about the map. There was one for you, but I was… well.…" He flexed his hips, a little embarrassed. "I was *inside* you, so your rock was, well, shot through with *me*, I guess, and it… it was glowing."

"Oh dear Goddess." Mack pushed himself up on his elbows and clenched hard to keep Jordan inside him. Then he closed his eyes and muttered something in Latin, three times.

Jordan felt a bonding then—a supernatural bonding, not just the emotional connection that had gotten deeper and stronger every time he and Macklin touched. With a little sigh, Macklin fell back against the bed and went limp, allowing Jordan to slide out of him and to the side. He raised an arm above both their heads and rolled so he could put his other hand on Macklin's hip, their sweating bodies intimately close. Macklin pushed up and grabbed the sheet and comforter, pulled it over their shoulders, and the illusion of protection, of the two of them in a perfect bubble of time, was complete.

But when Jordan closed his eyes, he could sense the magic, and it wasn't an illusion.

"So," he said, glad his voice didn't give away the sudden fear in his belly.

"That was my father's study," Macklin said—and he *did* sound afraid. "He's obviously been searching for me, and you found him when he was open and vulnerable, probably looking at the stones on his map."

Jordan frowned. "Wait—I found *him*?"

Macklin smiled a little, touching Jordan's mouth softly. "You're so strong," he said, sounding helpless and happy about it. "I knew it when I got pulled through your portal. The lot of you didn't even know you'd made it. They're next-level magic, but your determination—"

"That's everybody, Macklin. You've seen it."

Macklin shook his head. "I know you say that, but Jordan, it's your love, your determination that's brought everybody this far. Do you know what the first spell a wizard learns is?"

Jordan shook his head. "Got nothin'."

"Lighting candles! Because if a wizard child can't light candles, they get fostered out somewhere else. They have no magic. But you can light candles. Everybody in your coven can. And at first I thought, 'What the hell is in the water?' and then I realized what it was, watching your morning and evening rituals. *You willed them to.* You can do it—first, second try?"

"Fifth. I'm still back on 'fostered out.'"

Macklin's mouth twisted. "That's because your fathers love you. But yes, if the whole breeding program doesn't work, we get fostered someplace without magic or sent to work with the household staff. It's—"

"Deplorable!" Jordan cried, and Macklin touched his shoulder reassuringly.

"It's not how you'd work in a million million years," he agreed. He leaned forward to kiss Jordan then, and Jordan's anxiety melted a little with the touch of lips. Macklin could do that to him, but Macklin could also make him feel like he could move mountains.

"So your father was looking for *you*," Jordan said, needing to get this conversation back underneath him.

"And you must have sensed that. After orgasm, your brain tends to clear out and stop getting in its own way. Dad was searching for me, so you were drawn to him."

Jordan had a sudden, terrifying thought. "Do you think I was… uhm, visible?" He grimaced. "In, uh, all my, uh…?"

Macklin's grin had more than a touch of evil in it. "I think Father probably had a very clear idea of what we were doing, yes," he said. His smile faded. "And I think we're going to have to be very, very careful for a few more days out."

They *had* been being careful—in the extreme. Jordan and Macklin had been reading spell books, casting practice cantrips, doing alchemical equivalencies the same way Jordan had done physics experiments in college. But the only spell—the *only* full spell—they'd cast had been the morning and evening ritual, and that was always with the coven.

"What makes you think he'll stop looking for you after that?" Jordan asked, mortified when he yawned. They'd been running full out, every day, but he and Macklin had also been stealing time every night to make love. Of course there was always a piper to pay for things like lost sleep, and Jordan was paying it now.

"Because the presence will be gone, and your friends will be free. The danger of a wizard intervention will have passed, and he won't know enough to care about your coven," Mack told him on his own yawn. "Did you set the clock?"

Jordan nodded and rolled over to turn the knob on the little white plastic clock, making sure it was set for 7:15 a.m.

"Done," he said, wrapping Macklin securely in his embrace.

He woke up alone and naked, covered in a thick woolen blanket, sleeping on the carpet in front of the black stone hearth.

From far away—so very far away—he heard the ring of his alarm clock, but neither Macklin nor his bedroom at the witch's cottage nor the cul-de-sac were anywhere to be seen.

He's Not There

MACKLIN blinked his eyes open just enough to watch Jordan disappear.

Shit.

Shit.

He didn't bother calling out for Jordan. And in spite of the fact that every instinct, every *synapse*, was screaming for him to open a portal, grab Jordan, and jerk him back to where he belonged, Macklin *couldn't*.

For one, the only reason his father had been able to find Jordan was because of his proximity to Mack himself. Everybody else in the coven was safe—safe from Mack's father's interference, safe from getting their powers stripped, safe from being on the wizard's radar forever. He and Jordan had worked hard to make it so, and Mack had fallen into the embrace of Jordan's family so easily, so *thoroughly*, that he couldn't bear to think of what his father could do to the little family he'd become so close to.

Portals—two of them—would also take all of Macklin's energy, and he was charging up for the big spell on Samhain. So was Jordan, for that matter. To drain them both now, when with any luck Mack could call his father on the *phone* and have Alistair send him back on his *own* energy reserve, wasn't prudent.

But the big thing that held Macklin back was the entire reason they were waking up early in the first place—the morning ritual.

At this point, the little group of hedge witches getting up in the morning and returning in the evening was the only thing keeping the macabre happenings of the cul-de-sac from completely enveloping the surrounding neighborhoods. The presence in the house—now denied what had been a steady diet of self-deprecation and abnegation—was making a truly herculean effort to send all the houses for miles around into a land of warped realities, where all the birds flew upside down, crows were dive-bombing on command, owls chased the cats if they were unwary, and turkeys threatened revolt at the drop of a hat. There were snakes *everywhere*, and while most Northern California snakes were completely harmless, the occasional rattlesnake would slither by on the sidewalk, and the little dog didn't get walked anymore without first getting *carried* to where the influence of the cul-de-sac ended.

Which was getting farther and farther away from the epicenter of the witch's cottage.

Even if Macklin hadn't felt duty bound to protect Jordan's family, he would have had a magic user's duty to protect the world from the presence, and that meant taking Jordan's place at the ritual.

But it didn't mean he wasn't building up a huge, angry head of steam by the time he stomped across the paving stones, giving a slight nod as obeisance to the Nine and then smiling grimly at the others who were waiting for him.

"Wait," Kate yawned groggily, hauling a giant coat around her pug-dog pajamas. "Where's Jordan?"

Macklin didn't even want to look at them, standing in their PJs and trying to wake up enough to pull magic from the toes of exhaustion.

"My father kidnapped him through a portal when the alarm went off," he said, jaw clenched. "And I want to go after him so bad but—"

"But we gotta do this first," Josh said, suddenly awake. "I get it." He glanced up to where Simon and Lachlan waited. Sometimes, when somebody was busy, they got called in to make a full complement of five. Macklin was there, most of the time, but they'd kept him out of the ritual specifically not to attract his father's attention, and that seemed moot now. "Guys, come over here. We're gonna need seven without J."

"Where's Jordan?" Lachlan asked, slipping his hand inside Bartholomew's.

"My father zapped him through a portal when the alarm rang," Macklin told him, hating hearing it all over again.

"And you're *here*?" Simon asked. "You let him go?"

Macklin stared at him. "You of all people should know why I didn't follow him," he snapped. "We have got bigger things to deal with right now." His chin wobbled. "And then I can look for him." He glanced around the circle at Jordan's friends and felt the wrongness of leading the ritual. Dammit, Jordan should *be here*.

"I hate to admit it," Bartholomew said, sounding hurt and scared, "but Macklin's right." He checked over his shoulder to where the squirrels were beginning to wake up. They'd been waking up closer and closer to darkness, and each time they did, they started to break the bonds of their infinity-symbol march and berate the turkeys and the crows instead. There was violence brewing between the mammals and the birds that threatened to break out at any time if they let their guard slip.

"Yeah," Simon said, "but Jordan!"

"Well, I'd be honored if you let me lead this time," Macklin asked formally, relieved when everybody nodded. He squeezed Bartholomew on his left and Kate on his right and took a deep breath, trying to call up a cantrip that would ease people's minds at the same time it empowered them.

Jordan was so good at that.

"How about 'Together we are stronger than fear,'" Alex proposed when Mack's mind threatened a giant blank.

Mack smiled at him gratefully. "That's perfect," he said. "Thrice times thrice for nine—all of us individually, then together for the last two times."

They all nodded.

"I'll start." He paused, then recited, "Together we are stronger than fear."

As he said the words, he felt something tremendous echoing from his chest, as though his magic had been hit with a tuning fork, and in front of him a column of lapis-lazuli colored light built, strong enough to attract attention from a mile away. Then Kate went, her light amethyst colored, and so on, around the circle, everybody's strength represented by the color that best showed it. As they repeated the small spell together the first time, the light began to whirl, and as they said it the second, it exploded, bathing the neighborhood in wholesome sunshine, chasing back the abnormal purple light that built up between rituals.

Macklin felt the power scatter, healing the neighborhood once again, and he sagged a little, breaking the hand link and rubbing the back of his neck.

"Okay," he said as though the ritual had never happened. "I have an idea, but first, I call my father and see if I can't talk reason to him. And if that doesn't work—"

"What?" Alex demanded.

"If that doesn't work, we open a portal with our next ritual and hope my father doesn't find us between sunset tonight and sunrise tomorrow."

Simon closed his eyes and shuddered. Hell, they *all* did. "Macklin," he said delicately, "I think—and of course you all work the magic, I'm just an extra body here—but I think it might be safer, given how scary you've painted your family to be, to open a portal at tomorrow morning's ritual, skip the evening ritual, then dive right into the spell for Samhain at midnight. Let the magic take over while we're setting up. Unless there's a magical reason I don't know about…." He held up both hands.

Macklin let out a long sigh. "I'll think about it," he promised. "We didn't want to leave the neighborhood unprotected in the six hours between dark and midnight, remember? I mean, it's Halloween—we don't want kids to run into rattlesnakes and scary squirrels and such as they're trick-or-treating."

Simon grimaced. "I had forgotten," he said, sounding surprised. "Imagine that. Distracted from Halloween by a bunch of witches. You have to admit it's funny."

They all let out a tired chuckle, and Macklin felt a little better.

"Let me talk to my father," he said quietly, "and then we'll figure out what has to be done."

Macklin hated to have an audience for the conversation with his father. On the one hand, it seemed unbearably private. But on the other, this wasn't only the fate of his lover at stake. This was the fate of this tiny, devoted coven of friends, and Macklin was responsible for them as well.

They deserved to be in on the conversation and to hear what they were up against.

He put the phone on speaker and then set it on the kitchen table while he and the others ranged around it.

"I'll try to warn you if I'm going to lie outright," he said softly. "But I'll tell you right now, if he asks if I'm alone, I'm going to say yes. Maybe put the dog in one of the bedrooms?"

Everybody nodded soberly, and Alex grabbed a couple of dog treats and the dog bed, then called for Glinda, who trotted happily after him.

Alex returned and took a seat right when Macklin hit Call.

"Hello?" his father said uncertainly. "I'm sorry, I don't recognize this number."

"Then maybe you should call it before you kidnap my boyfriend," Macklin said, voice dripping in acid. "It would certainly make me happier to be your son."

"Is he your boyfriend?" his father asked. "I was not aware."

Around the table, people's eyes bulged out, and everybody shook out their hands or arms if they'd been resting on the wood, but nobody made a sound.

"You lying asshole," Macklin charged, furious that quickly. "Try again."

"I have no idea what—"

This time Macklin let out a yelp so everybody else could release a breath.

"Father, if you're going to keep lying, I'm going to hang up and build a portal and rip Jordan right out of your hands." He was clenching his fists as he said it, and he realized they were glowing. Nobody at the table batted an eyelash, and it hit him—hard—that he was angry enough and powerful enough to do exactly what he threatened.

"I—"

"*No lies!*" Macklin roared, feeling the table building up charge.

"Your boyfriend is fine," Alistair snapped churlishly, and when the table didn't react, everybody sagged in relief.

"Finally," Macklin told him. "The fucking truth. Is he clothed?"

"Yes—"

Everybody bit their lips and glared at Macklin, who barked, "*For fuck's sake, give him some pants. Now!*"

And then he hung up.

"Holy wow," Lachlan muttered, wrapping his arm around Bartholomew's shoulders and blowing on both their hands. "What an asshole."

"Yeah," Macklin agreed. "I'm starting to see why I went for seventeen years without speaking to him."

"What do we do now?" Bartholomew asked.

"We wait," Simon told them, no uncertainty in his voice at all.

Macklin grimaced but nodded. "He's not in any physical discomfort. I suspect Alistair was trying to show his dominance. Alistair knows my number. He'll call back."

It was Josh who gave them some much-needed humor. "Heh heh… was he really naked when he got zapped over to your dad?"

Heat flashed in Macklin's cheeks. "Yes."

"Good. He'll be madder'n a wet hen. Your poor dad. You're pissed and Jordan's probably nuclear. I don't see this ending well for him."

"What's our worst-case scenario?" Alex asked, sounding troubled.

"I open a portal and drag him back, and you all have to do Samhain without me," Macklin said. "Or at least with me at half speed. I'm still not 100 percent after that day last week."

"Can we do it?" Lachlan asked, and Macklin thought about it seriously, coming up with the same conclusion he'd been arriving at all week.

"Yes," he said. "But…." He bit his lip thoughtfully, his eyes darting to the wall of the living room closest to Dante and Cully's house. "It would be easier if we had their help."

They'd been sending two people at a time in, once a day, to keep Dante and Cully up-to-date on what was happening and to move their stuff out. At the moment, they were down to mattresses on the floor. Nobody had wanted to ask if they'd been sharing a mattress and blankets or sleeping separate—not only was it a violation of privacy, but it felt wrong. Whatever fate awaited Dante and Cully when they'd been recovered from limbo, it was very much *their* fate. The coven would love them in whatever incarnation they took when they emerged from their free-floating pocket in space and time.

So far, the men had been absent every time someone had visited. Macklin thought if they could at least be aware of, if not participate in, the ritual on Samhain evening, they could forge part of the path that would bring them back to the reality in which all of their friends existed.

Macklin could feel the hole the two of them had left every time they gathered for the morning and evening ritual. He anticipated meeting the men when they weren't disappearing and appearing randomly in the middle of a conversation.

"I don't know what more we can do," Bartholomew said softly. "I'll try leaving Post-its on their food again, but I don't know what they're seeing."

"I'll help you, Barty." Alex winked at him, and Macklin felt another tug in his chest. They were two men who were meant to be brothers but never lovers— the antithesis of Dante and Cully. There was a symmetry to that.

"Okay," Macklin said on a breath. "We won't depend on their help—we can't. However this plays out, without Jordan or without me, we need to treat getting them like diving for puppies in a well."

Barty and Alex both nodded and went to deliver food and Post-its to their refrigerator, boyfriends in tow, and Macklin was left at the kitchen table with Kate and Josh.

"You look like a man who needs cookies," Kate announced out of nowhere.

"I do?" Macklin gave her a weak smile.

"Well, *I* do, so we should share."

They were in the middle of their second cookie—well, Josh's fourth—before the phone rang again.

"Is he clothed yet?" Macklin demanded.

"Macklin." Jordan said quickly, "do whatever you need to without me. I'll find my own way home."

Macklin heard a grunt and the sound of flesh hitting flesh and Alistair snapping, "Jesus, kid, you got a lot of fucking balls!"

"Love you, Mack!" Jordan shouted. "Get it done!"

And then the line went dead.

Macklin stared at the phone, the cookies turning to ashes in his mouth as he tried to find the spit to swallow.

"Did you hear what he said?" Macklin asked Kate and Josh, who had both moved to his shoulders to offer support.

"Yeah," Josh said. "He said he loved you."

Macklin's breath caught. He'd been thinking about the "Get it done!" and the "I'll find my own way home!" because that spoke of two things—trust that Macklin would take care of Jordan's people and confidence that he could get home with or without Alistair's help.

But until Josh spoke, he hadn't been aware that the one thing—the thing that gave him the courage and the hope to keep going even though Jordan wasn't there by his side—was that Jordan loved him as much as he loved Jordan.

Macklin nodded, keenly aware that Josh had put his finger on the pulse of the situation once again. "My father will never know what hit him," he said, voice thick but his strength building. "I'm going to meet him halfway."

Suspicious Minds

JORDAN stared at the remains of Alistair Quintero's cell phone on the black hearth of the fireplace and chuckled, feeling mean.

Macklin hadn't been kidding about his father being a dick.

JORDAN had awakened on the hearth naked and covered in a blanket. He'd taken his time standing up, making sure the blanket was wrapped well and that his dignity was intact. The impression he'd gotten from Mack was that Alistair cared deeply about the way things appeared and the way they played out. Bound by tradition—and by a love of power—catching Jordan as he slept, or worse, in the act of making love, had been a power play of the basest sort.

Jordan didn't really give a shit about this man's opinion now. Power play *rejected*. Jordan had been doing grown-ups' business in his own goddamned home, and if this man didn't like his business or him, he needed to act like a grown-up himself and broach the subject like a goddamned adult.

Instead he glanced around, seeing the same room he'd visited the night before in Macklin's arms. Spotting the giant teak desk with a world map etched into the surface and stained over so as to be permanent, he stared at the stones scattered on top.

Most of them were in the middle of a place he knew to be wooded and isolated in upstate New York, very close to the Canadian border. Jordan closed his eyes, allowing his blood to thrum in time with the elements, and while there was no window nearby, he could feel the building energy of midmorning as opposed to the sleepy clarity of sunrise.

Yeah—he'd been yanked 3,000 miles away from his home so he could confront his boyfriend's father buck naked and asleep.

Fucking. Awesome.

Carefully, he examined the stones on the board and spotted one on the West Coast—a lapis lazuli pebble, or it had been, but it was more complicated than that now. It was still shot through with sapphire, the two layered and intertwined in a way not found in nature but definitely found in this little rock. And there were shaded parts of the lapis lazuli, mysterious parts, smoke-colored, holding the bright heart of the stone to itself.

Very carefully, Jordan picked the stone up and clutched it in his palm.

"Put that back" came an older voice—a *snide* voice.

"Put *me* back," Jordan snapped over his shoulder. "You had no business pulling me from my bed. Put me back."

"You had no business seducing my son!" Alistair Quintero replied. It had to be him; the resemblance to Macklin was unmistakable, even with the graying black hair and the beard. His eyes, though, weren't piercing blue—not like Macklin's. They were, instead, smoke-colored, a dark blue, a blue of secrets and no light.

Jordan gave a harsh bark of laughter. "*I* seduced *him*? I'm sorry, but have you *met* your son? Believe me, he's more than capable of getting anybody in his bed he wants. I was lucky enough to be on his list."

Alistair blinked rapidly, and to Jordan's grim amusement, he could see the older man was *really* uncomfortable at hearing this much about his son's sex life. Well, tough. Jordan's fathers and his Aunt Bella had pretty much coached him in how to have a sex life without seeming like too much of a freak, and Jordan gave no fucks about this man's embarrassment. Alistair had zapped him in *naked* to make *Jordan* uncomfortable. Who gave a shit how he felt?

"You didn't know your son was bi? Well, now you know. Maybe check in with him more than once every eighteen years."

"You don't know anything about my relationship with my son—"

Jordan snorted. "I know if my parents don't hear from me every eighteen *hours* they assume I'm dead in a ditch. In college I kept a collection of cute pictures on my phone so I could text them and they wouldn't be driving forty miles through traffic to check my pulse while I slept. At this point, you'll have to do a lot more to impress me with your parenting style, trust me."

Alistair gaped at him.

"By the way, is there a *bathroom* around this place? You pulled me here right before I was supposed to wake up, and I have to piss like a racehorse." Jordan sent a silent thanks to Josh for giving him that expression—and the chutzpah to use it while Alistair was so surprised he could barely talk.

Alistair waved his hand in a little bit of showmanship, and where there had existed only an alcove in the corner of the vast study, there was now a door.

"Through there, to the right," Alistair told him coldly. "Talk to nobody, and don't try to escape. You're—"

"In the middle of the woods near the northeastern United States," Jordan told him dryly. "I hear you." And with that, perversely, he dropped the blanket, because cold or not, he didn't feel like huddling in it while he wandered this asshole's home.

"You're going to go out there like that?" Alistair sounded scandalized.

Prick.

"Well, if you'd wanted me to have some manners, you could have waited until I got dressed before you zapped me into your study, right?"

"I thought you'd be wearing pajamas!"

Jordan snorted. "Your son wasn't," he said and swanned out.

He found the bathroom, which was almost bigger than the entire cottage he'd been living in for the last year and a half and done almost entirely in black and off-white marble. After he used the facilities, he took his time to wash up extensively. He still wore Macklin on his skin. He'd finished up and was in the process of brushing his teeth with his finger and some toothpaste found in the cabinet when there was a knock on the door.

Jordan fought the desire to grab a towel, because— again—fuck this guy, and got there right as the doorknob was being turned.

He flung open the door in all his glory and stared down Alistair Quintero, who held a folded pile of clothes for him.

Jordan looked at him and then took in the trousers— wide at the hips and short in the leg or he hadn't been ordering special since he was a gangly teenager—and a henley T-shirt, too narrow in the shoulders and short in the waist.

He sized up Alistair's proportions and knew these must have been his castoffs.

"If it wasn't so goddamned cold in here, I'd almost rather go naked," he said and then slammed the door.

Thirty seconds later he opened it—the clothes exactly as ill-fitting as he'd imagined they would be— and stalked toward the study. Behind him he had an impression of a vast home, big enough that it felt like a hotel, decorated in Vermont ski-lodge style, with big oaken beams and sunken dining rooms, with rich flowered area rugs and great bay windows. Pretty, he knew, but he had no intention of exploring *or* of getting cozy here.

In his entire life—even when he'd dreamed of magic and hadn't known the nuts and bolts—he'd never imagined opening up a portal and just... just *going* somewhere else. But that was before he'd created one for Macklin and been yanked through one himself. Granted, the first portal for Macklin had been unintentional, but that's part of what made it possible. He and the others had *wanted*—they'd needed help, and Jordan had needed *someone*—so badly that first night, as they'd cast that spell. They hadn't expected magic to reach out and snag Macklin by the scruff of the neck, but every day, every *minute*, with Macklin had convinced Jordan to trust in magic, trust in fate, trust in *Macklin*, that Mack's involvement with Jordan and his friends was the best possible thing to have happened since Jordan had first walked into Helen's cottage and decided he wanted to be a witch.

Jordan trusted in that want now. He knew what a spell was, he knew what power was, and he knew how to wield it. His want would open a portal and bring him home, but he also knew by watching Macklin that it would sap him of strength. His coven needed his strength, and they definitely needed his protection.

Macklin had put a seal around their neighborhood—Jordan trusted that. But they would want to get him back before midnight tomorrow, California time, and during the rituals was their only opportunity to do that without breaking the seal or clueing Macklin's father in to where they were. Macklin had said that the rituals were common enough among practitioners that even a big power surge wouldn't be able to be detected, not even by Macklin's father.

Jordan needed to bide his time and find out what Macklin's father wanted. He'd be getting home soon enough.

Furious but knowing better than to antagonize his host needlessly, Jordan stalked after Alistair as he led the way back to his study.

As they rounded the corner, he noticed another man—a younger, softer version of Macklin but with brown hair instead of raven's-wing black—following behind them. He held his finger to his lips, and Jordan didn't say a word as they slipped into the study and the wall appeared behind them.

Jordan took a few steps forward toward the desk, keeping his eyes on Alistair and not on the uninvited guest in the corner.

"The clothes suck," he said by way of opening. "Thanks for nothing."

Alistair's jaw dropped. "You are clothed—"

"You summoned me out of nowhere, naked. Give me one good reason I should be grateful for anything you do."

"I'm the only way you can get back to your home," Alistair told him, like Jordan was stupid not to know this.

"Are you?" Jordan asked, arms folded. "*Are* you?"

Behind Alistair, the stranger in the corner smirked. "He's got you there, Father."

Alistair turned and glared. "Josue? What are you doing here?"

"I felt Macklin here last week," Josue said, eyes hard. "I *felt* him here. And you always forget that we're wizards too. We know summoning spells for things

with our own name on them. You kept his letters to me
in your desk drawer, Alistair. My brother *wrote* to me.
And you think that doesn't matter?"

"This has nothing to do with that—"

"It has everything to do with that," Jordan
said, heart aching for Josue and Macklin. Macklin's
childhood had been so lonely. If he'd had one person
to confide in and that person had been blocked from
him, that must have broken his heart. "Have you
learned nothing? Your son won't speak to you, so
you confiscate his letters. That doesn't work, so you
kidnap him. *That* doesn't work, so you kidnap his
boyfriend. And none of this is making him love you.
After enough failure, you should know when to quit.
You can't keep me here against my will."

"What, because you're a *hedge* witch? You think I
can't smell essential oils all over you?"

Jordan smirked. "No, sir, that's not what you smell
all over me."

He let that little bomb hang in the air, enjoying
Josue's snort of appreciation.

"Don't be vulgar," Alistair enunciated.

"Don't be condescending."

"I can strip your powers as you stand," Alistair
threatened, pulling out his phone. "And that's exactly
what I'm going to tell my son I will do unless he gives
up this stupid infatuation with you and comes home to
be with his family."

"I *am* his family," Jordan said without blinking.
His entire attention was focused on that phone, though,
because if nothing else, he and Macklin needed to be
on the same page.

Alistair hit the number, and Jordan vaulted the desk so smoothly he didn't displace a single pebble, crashed into Alistair, and grabbed the phone.

"Macklin, do whatever you need to without me," Jordan ordered. "I'll find my own way home."

Alistair's roundhouse to the eye was painful but expected. "Jesus, kid, you got a lot of fucking balls!" He snatched the phone while Jordan was trying to stay upright.

Jordan steadied himself on the desk, shouting, "Love you, Mack! Get it done!"

Alistair pitched the phone at the hearth like a toddler and snarled in frustration and anger.

JORDAN looked at the shattered piece of electronics and then back to Alistair Quintero. "Go ahead and try to strip my powers," he said evenly, although his heart broke when he said it. "Your son will never come back here. I've been here ten minutes, and my anger is eating me alive. You don't get him for the rest of his life. No way. He's got so much love to give. You're so stupid. You could have had… I don't know. Laughter. Fun. Kindness. All the things I have with my family. But you got this insanely tacky home—"

"Tacky!" Alistair gasped, but Jordan ignored him and refused to comment on his father's beautiful home with the open-area living room flanked by the elegant curve of two hand-carved wooden staircases and richly colored carpeting.

"I'm sure it's great for *Wizard's Compound Digest* or something," Jordan dismissed, "but it's never been a home. I would rather live without magic than live without Macklin, especially if that means he has to live in this dump. So you do what you want to me. I'll get out, somehow, and Macklin will never, ever come to you."

And that was it. He must have really pissed Alistair Quintero off that time, because Jordan felt it, a scouring desert wind, hitting him full force in the chest, trying to pull his skin from his bones, and—Jordan knew it—his magic from his heart.

But Jordan was angry for Macklin, he was terrified for his coven, and he was *furious* with this man for thinking he could strip Jordan of something he was good at, he was proud of, and that he used every day to make the world a sweeter, kinder place.

He turned his head so the sand wouldn't block his mouth and cried, "Let this ill wind blow your own harm into your heart!"

And nobody—nobody—was more surprised than he was when the wind abruptly shifted direction, knocking all of Alistair's people pieces off the top of his desk and snapping his head back, forcing him to stumble into his chair.

He screamed, and for a moment, Jordan could see flakes of obsidian pulled from his body, threatening to rip away in the hurricane of magic-stripping wind. As Jordan watched, Alistair began fumbling for words, and the obsidian started to merge with him again. Jordan steadied his feet, shoring up his magic and his fury for another round.

Only to find himself suddenly in a wooded clearing, already dusted with snow.

Josue was in front of him, leaning forward, hands on his knees, breathing hard.

"What in the hell—"

"Portals," Josue panted. "Father and Macklin can do them like snapping fingers. A little hard on those of us who aren't insanely talented, you know?"

Jordan laughed, his chest and his magic still ready for bear but his anger easing up a little.

"Why did you do that?" he asked, moving forward to help Josue stand.

"Because my brother wrote to me," Josue said, a sad smile on his lips. "He wanted to be brothers." That smile twisted, and his eyes—blue like Mack's—grew red-rimmed and shiny. "Growing up in this place? I needed a brother. So bad." He shook his head. "How dare Alistair? Seriously. Just… how dare he?"

Jordan nodded. "Yeah, fuck that guy," he agreed. "So, uhm… what now?"

"Well, Father will be able to find me in about an hour, I reckon. It'll take him that long to put together all the things on the table. And he's going to be pissed. So, uhm…." Josue sighed and prepared to step out of his brown loafers. His entire outfit, from Nordic sweater to khaki-colored slacks, screamed "father on a ski vacation." He eyed Jordan. "You look like a size, what? Twelve?"

"Thirteen," Jordan said dryly. "I won't fit. Do you have any cash and, I don't know, some directions to the next strip mall?"

Josue pulled out his wallet—and about $200. "It's not spelled or anything. Nobody can track it. And the strip mall is about a mile east. The road is about half a mile in that direction." He stepped out of his loafers for real and stripped off his socks. "Here—they'll protect you from stickers and pebbles, at least. I'm sorry. I… if my car wasn't five miles in the opposite direction, I'd lend you that."

Jordan chuckled and took the money and the socks, gratefully putting the one in his pocket and the other on his feet. "Well, then," he said with a shrug. "I've got some walking to do." He sobered and stuck out his hand. "Thank you, Josue. I'll tell Macklin about this. Give him a week or two—he'll be in touch."

Josue smiled softly. "Well, if Alistair doesn't strip *my* powers, I'll be here."

"Well, if he does, your brother's address is in Carson City right now." Jordan rattled off Macklin's business number—he'd gotten to talk to Macklin's partner once or twice in the last week, and Billy would pass on the information. It wasn't that he didn't trust Josue; it was that he didn't trust Alistair not to *follow* Josue. "You talk to Billy, and Mack will make sure he takes care of you."

Josue nodded. "Thank you. I...." He stuck his hand out. "I'm Josue Quintero, and I'm really happy to meet you."

"I'm Jordan," he said. "And give me two weeks and I'll introduce myself much better, I promise."

Another nod. "You're protecting someone?" he said, eyes narrowed cannily.

"Mostly Macklin," Jordan said truthfully. "But once he says to trust you completely, I will."

"Fair enough." Josue straightened. "Now hurry!"

Jordan set off through the woods then, sticking to deer paths when he could find them. When he got to the road, he headed east, mindful of the travelers and the sometimes icy roads. He was freezing himself, but he kept going, one eye on the sky. As he walked, he tried to find his center, his magical source with his family. Not because he wanted to contact them—not now—but because he was biding his time.

Waiting for sunset, Pacific Time.

He had a plan.

THE walk was uncomfortable to say the least, and he was grateful for the thick brown socks, right up until they developed holes and he had to throw them away. He was irritated, footsore, and damned cold by the time he found the strip mall, but he was alive, and he'd tried a tiny cantrip to warm his toes as he'd walked the last quarter mile, and it had worked.

Warm toes equaled a big win in the magic department, and he was grateful.

The strip mall was better than he could have hoped for. Josue's money bought a lot in terms of shoes, sweats, a burner phone, and some sundries at a Walmart. And when he was dressed and had thrown Alistair's clothes in a dumpster, he had enough left over to sit and eat and watch the clock.

He didn't need to.

The sunset on the East Coast didn't thrum in his blood, but he felt it. Knew it was happening. Checked his phone and set an alarm for three hours minus fifteen minutes as it happened.

Then he bought himself a paperback and another cup of coffee and waited.

Before his phone even went off, his entire body began to twitch. This was *his* sun, over *his* sky, and it was going to set in the world's oldest dance between darkness and light.

Jordan set out behind the strip mall, which was backed by half-naked trees and even a stream about fifty yards behind where the pavement for the auto bay ended.

Perfect. He ran into the trees, looking carefully about for homeless encampments, and was relieved to see none. So funny—a brief jog behind a bustling retail outlet and here he was, where vulnerable limbs stood in stark relief against a harvest moon under an unfamiliar sky.

Working quickly, he found a bare spot where the stars and the moon peeked through the trees and pulled out some of his purchases from his pocket.

Sage, basil, thyme, rosemary, and cinnamon— he put a small bit of each herb equidistant in a circle, and then, using the pour spout of a container of salt, he created a pentagram with each of the ingredients at its point. Above each point, he placed a candle. Green for Alex, amber for Bartholomew, purple for Kate, aquamarine for Josh, and gold and blue for Macklin. He knew Simon and Lachlan were probably in the circle too, but he didn't have a candle for them, and a seven-pointed star was damned hard to make with any sort of skill without a compass.

But Simon and Lachlan would give power to the circle on the other side of the portal. What mattered on Jordan's side was his connection to the people there, and it was strongest with those represented in his circle.

Careful not to disturb the salt, he stepped to the inside of the pentagram and closed his eyes. He didn't have to check the time on his burner phone to know it was close.

He could feel it.

Eyes still closed, he envisioned his coven, the people he loved and the people he was growing to love, and he felt their need for him.

Felt their want.

Felt their connection to him—even Simon and Lachlan—like strings being wound to pull him from this faraway place.

The strings wrapped around him, from his extremities to his limbs to his core, and he was cocooned in their love, in their care, and echoing in his head, he heard their chant.

As one we stand against the dark, as many we pray for the light.

One at a time they said the chant, and Jordan waited, waited, through seven singular voices, and then, when it was time to repeat the chant two more times, he joined in, the pull of their love growing stronger and stronger.

In the end, he was shouting by himself, the third time, as the crisp fall air blurred around him, the stars shifting in their courses, the world buckling under his feet.

As one we stand against the dark, as many we pray for the light.

And then he was home, Macklin in his arms, his friends wrapping themselves around him, crying in joy, and all was right with the world.

(Your Love Keeps Lifting Me) Higher and Higher

MACKLIN woke up to Jackie Wilson singing about love lifting him higher and felt a moment's sadness for the house.

"You know," he said, his voice a whisper in the dark, "presences start out as positive things, then go wrong. Humility and a willingness to learn are good qualities. If we leave, I wouldn't mind taking a few things with me."

He listened intently for a moment, reaching to where Jordan lay next to him, exhausted by finding a portal in thin air and generally surviving his encounter with Macklin's father. Jordan's even breathing and warm body reassured him for the millionth time that they were doing the right thing.

And then, to his surprise, the old house did too, as the opening drum clicks of the Monkees' "I'm a Believer" rolled quietly through the house.

"Just, you know," he added hastily, "maybe not quite so pervasive."

And the music quieted, leaving barely enough volume for Macklin to hear the joy in it. Jordan mumbled and rolled over in his arms.

"Time yet?" he asked.

Macklin glanced at the windup clock, glow-in-the-dark hands telling him they had two more hours.

"No, love," he murmured. "Get your rest. You'll need it."

"All I need is you," Jordan said, and pulled him a little closer. Their bodies were sated. They'd had their own private reunion after Jordan had been hugged and loved—and fed, and debriefed—by everybody else, but Macklin felt the thrum of need still running under his skin.

He thought with a little bit of wonder that he might feel this pulsing in his blood for the rest of his life.

"Me too," he murmured. "I still don't understand how you did it, J."

He'd never had to trust somebody like that before. Jordan had told him to get it done. Macklin had assumed, and rightly so, he meant the ritual, taking care of the coven, still planning for the future. Jordan said he'd find his way back home.

Macklin had never imagined he meant he would ride their ritual like a portal, letting it summon him like it had summoned Macklin, except with the intent on Jordan's side.

The amount of will—and strength and skill—it took to do this was stunning. Jordan probably could summon his own portals out of thin air with relatively little training and only his own determination and need.

The possibilities were staggering, but at the same time they simply indicated everything Macklin had known about his lover from the very beginning.

Intense, dedicated, protective.

Full of questions, a little self-doubt, and love.

Always, always, love.

These were the qualities that made up Jordan Bryne, and Macklin was all in for him: heart, mind, body, soul.

As he lay there in the wee hours of the morning, he knew—as though he'd seen the future, he knew—that they would succeed that night. On Samhain midnight, they would free the last two members of the coven from the presence, and the coven, as a whole, could have its new start on the wooded hillsides that made up their new home.

And he and Jordan Bryne would be making that start together.

"Macklin, I can hear you thinking," Jordan murmured.

"Good," Macklin told him, his voice still at a whisper. "Because I've got only good thoughts."

He fell asleep to Jordan's gentle chuckle, looking forward to the dawn.

I Say a Little Prayer

IN a million years, Jordan wouldn't have thought they could do this.

Simon's property in Jackson, adjoined with Lachlan's, formed the shape of a five-pointed star, with a gentle rise on each point. The property surrounded by the small hills was in various stages of growth—some thick woods on Kate and Josh's point, a small forest on Lachlan's point of the area, and almost all plain meadow on what Dante and Cully's hillside would be.

But none of the woodland was so thick it could obscure the bonfire on the peak of each hill.

Preparation had been key. Simon had been going to clear out his property anyway, and he'd paid the workers to build firepits in six strategic places—one of them in front of his mansion, one behind Lachlan's house, three more on the other hills.

And one in the very middle of the star.

They'd arranged for some basic things at every bonfire site—sand, salt, gallons of water both blessed and unblessed, dinner, candles, thread, and bundles of herbs. The herbs were much like the ones Jordan had used, tied with ten colored ribbons, one color for each member of the now-expanded coven—except for the center bundle. That hex bag was saved for Dante's and Cully's colors, Dante's and Cully's herbs, even stones—ruby for Dante, topaz for Cully—which were set around the bonfire pit for the two of them.

They'd spent all week practicing cantrips to put fires out on a moment's notice too. Getting their friends back while burning down Jackson was *not* in the plans.

Who would man which bonfire had been tricky, though.

Jordan was doing the bulk of the work, lighting them via magic, so the natural place for him to be was in the center. And they wanted somebody with power to be at each point.

Finally they'd decided that Simon and Alex needed to be manning the fire in front of Simon's great mansion, and Lachlan was coming along quickly enough to man his own. That left Bartholomew, Kate, and Josh to take care of the other fires, while Jordan and Macklin tended the great blaze in the center, both of them prepped with burn cream, blankets, aloe, and even more water in case things went really wrong.

And everybody had a cat.

True to Jordan's promise, after performing the evening ritual in the now-darkened cul-de-sac, he got in his car—packed with the last of the books from the witch's library—and opened the passenger door.

Six of the cats—including the giant gray fluffy one Jordan admired so much and the fierce little calico Josh loved—turned and padded over and leapt gracefully, one after the other, into the car, ranging themselves on the floor and seats of Jordan's compact hybrid.

The other three looked longingly after their friends, and Jordan called, "I'll be by tomorrow morning, if you like, and I can bring you with me then."

To a one the cats nodded modestly, twitching their tails, before returning their gaze to the center of the cul-de-sac in the darkening twilight.

"Awesome," Jordan told them. "I'll see you then. Wish us well tonight, okay?"

He saw their ears flicker and took it as a sign before closing the passenger door, pulling his seat belt on, and driving away.

The six cats who'd accompanied him remained bored and nonchalant through the forty-five-minute drive to Jackson that brought them all to everybody's new home.

Jordan was the last to arrive, and he saw that everybody else had lit electric lanterns in the fallen darkness. There were camp chairs and blankets at every site—and ice chests of water and sandwiches too. They had to purify the bonfire sites with salt and sage, then establish a pentacle at each site, with the bonfire in the middle. Jordan had decided to go with trenches and sand to make the pentagrams, and while Simon had arranged for the sand to be brought in to each place and the trenches dug, they couldn't fill them in with sand—mixed with salt—until after the purification. It was a lot of work to do between seven or so, when everybody arrived at the property, and a quarter till midnight, when everybody was going to get ready for Jordan to light the bonfires.

That's why there were sandwiches in the iceboxes. They were going to need fuel.

Jordan pulled to a stop in the clearing, far enough from the bonfire to be out of danger should anything go awry, but close enough to see Macklin was already there—and he'd already started digging. Jordan reached behind him and brought out the cat food and two of the bowls he'd been using for food and water and then turned to the cats on the seat.

"I, uh, will still feed you all if you like. I know there's coyotes and such out here, but I figure you're sort of badass. So, you know. I'll let you out and you guys go where you need to, and I'll get your friends tomorrow, okay?"

He was met by six pairs of eyes, ranging in color from gold to green to pale blue, that regarded him with quiet blinks.

What did he know? It's not like he spoke "cat."

He held the driver's side door open, and the cats filed out one by one, then looked at him expectantly as he set up a little food-and-water station by the pentagram. Macklin glanced up from where he was getting busy with the burning sage in the center of the pentagram and said, "Help me with the salt after this; then we can shovel in the sand and go help anyone who needs it."

Jordan nodded, conscious of the time, and got to work.

Three hours later, hot, sweaty, and sore, they took in their handiwork.

The pentagram, completed, surrounded the firepit, was lined with salt and filled with sand. Small hex bags filled with herbs and stones representing every member of the coven had been placed at the points, and black candles, representing the purity and the power of magic, sat with them.

They were telling the magic who their coven was and who they were as individuals, and they were appealing to its purity and power. Every one of them—every one—had learned something since the bollixed spell during the solstice had changed them.

Josh and Kate had learned that to have a future with each other, they had to plan for a future—not for a pageant.

Alex had learned that in order to have passion, he had to commit fully to the person he was with, and Simon had learned that the substance of a person was so much more important than their flash.

Bartholomew had learned that the only way to have faith in a lover was to have faith in himself, and Lachlan had learned that humility in the face of love was important in forging an unbreakable bond.

What had he learned? What had Macklin?

"What?" Macklin asked, pausing for a bottle of water. "Do you see anything we missed?"

"No," Jordan murmured, mentally going over the spell they'd laid. "I was thinking that every one of us has learned something important. I was wondering about your lesson—and trying to put words to my own."

Macklin laughed shortly.

"When you people ripped me out of time and space," he said, voice amused and arch, "I was riding through the desert, trying not to think of my family. I hate them, but I missed them too. I told you I'd been thinking about rewriting my life for a while, but I couldn't. I mean, you've met them. You can see why. But now…." He gave a winsome smile that made him appear younger—younger than Jordan and his friends, even. "Now I have people to protect, who would protect me too. I have family that cares for me. And I think even if you and I didn't work out, they would still be my friends."

Jordan nodded in understanding. "I would never take them away from you," he said softly.

"Thank you," Macklin said. He bumped Jordan's hot, sweaty shoulder with his own. "Don't take you away from me either."

Jordan gave him a shy smile. "Why would I want to do that?" he asked, meaning it. No reason at all to drive Macklin away. Macklin had become his heart.

"So what did *you* learn?" Macklin asked. They had to start personal preparations in a moment, but right now they had enough time in the chilly night to listen to the quiet and look at the shiny diamond scatter of stars above them. The air smelled of dust and oak, and a little like grapes—they were near wine country after all.

Jordan stared upward, allowed his soul to expand for a moment, see himself as he had been, see himself as he was now.

"I learned that I have power in this world," he said, eyes drifting closed. "That the things I've been given that I've always thought of as liabilities can sometimes be my strengths, if I allow them to be. And that I have a family I love too, and I need to trust them to help me when the weight of all that power, that responsibility, becomes too heavy."

He opened his eyes and peered at Macklin in the light of the nearby lantern. "I learned that there's nobody on earth I'd rather share my burden with than you."

Macklin leaned in to capture his mouth in a brief kiss, and a sharp "Meow!" pulled them apart. The familiars had all melted into the underbrush after they'd eaten—all but the big fluffy gray one who liked to sleep on their feet sometimes, who had decided they were his to oversee.

"Things to do," Jordan said, laughing. Then he sighed. "Do we really have to do this next part?"

Macklin had opened his mouth to answer when Jordan's phone buzzed in his pocket.

It was Bartholomew. "Jordan?"

"Yes?"

"Alex, Kate, and I were all wondering—do we really have to do this next part?"

"Yes!" Macklin called, loud enough for Bartholomew to hear him on his little hilltop, probably. "We need to be clean and naked and unashamed before our gods—tell them that. Now break out your bodywash, take off your clothes, and wet-wipe your pits!"

"Aw, jeez!" Bartholomew muttered. "Fine! We've got half an hour to showtime—I'll start the conference call in twenty-five minutes."

"You all have blankets until then?" Jordan asked, shivering.

"Yes, Jordan," Bartholomew answered patiently. "It's not the cold I'm worried about. It's some random stranger seeing me naked in the moonlight."

"No strangers, only friends," Jordan told him gently. "And some of us have seen each other's bits. It's okay."

"Not. Helping. Bye."

Barty ended the call, and Jordan moved over to the car, where he pulled out a reused milk carton full of pre-prepared sage, lavender, and sea salt wash, and then another one for Macklin. Two freshly laundered cloths were in the same box with the blankets, and Jordan looked at the SUV Macklin had driven. They'd kept Macklin's vehicle a little less packed, since—hopefully—they'd have two more people when they drove away. Macklin theorized that Dante and Cully would be exhausted and out of it if they came through a portal of both space and time, and they'd have to spend some time adjusting before Jordan and his friends could figure out which reality had settled into their memories. Jordan had consoled the coven with the thought that while it might be uncomfortable for *them*, it would probably be *overwhelming* for Dante and Cully. They had to keep their patience and their flexibility.

Just getting them back would be a victory. Whether or not they'd learned the lesson that was so clear to everybody else—well, that remained to be seen.

Another dive into the car to pull out thick full-length fleece robes and flip-flops for both of them and he and Macklin were ready.

"Remember the chant?" Macklin asked, unbuttoning his shirt.

"Yeah. Start now?"

Macklin nodded, and he and Jordan began to sing softly to the tune of "Yellow Rose of Texas."

I strip myself before the world
Stand naked on the earth
I cleanse myself of sin and pride
Am humble of my worth

I ask only to serve the world
To lend my talents there
Let my sincerity bring forth
The magic in the air

They repeated it as they stripped and folded their clothes, rinsed each other off using the blessed water, and then dried each other, shivering. From far away they could hear Lachlan's voice as he belted out his chant with more enthusiasm than tune, probably to keep Bartholomew from melting into the ground with embarrassment, and after a few verses, Josh's voice joined him.

Jordan and Macklin chuckled as they finished up their last stanza and wrapped themselves in their robes, stepping into the flip-flops at the same time.

"What do you want to bet they become best friends by Christmas," Macklin murmured.

"No bet," Jordan told him. "It's happened already."

And with that, they met eyes and stepped up to the giant pentagram built around the wood for the bonfire. Macklin brushed Jordan's hand with his own before walking around to the other side, and Jordan pulled the cell phone from the pocket of his robe and saw the group call was already buzzing.

He hit Call and Speaker so Macklin could hear.

"You guys ready?"

"Yeah" came the almost unanimous answer. Then Alex spoke, the quiet voice of reason they all treasured. "J, you're good to go? We could light our own candles, you know—"

"All of them together?" Macklin called. "No. Jordan lights the bonfires, because he's got the raw power, and I light the candles because I've got the finesse. You all concentrate on lending your power to the two of us—and on the words. It needs to feel like we're holding hands, even though we're far away, like when we felt Jordan before we made the portal together."

"Got it!" Alex said. "We ready?"

"I go first, and then we all join in," Jordan said. "We repeat it nine times and then hope for the best, starting on the count of midnight."

"That's twenty seconds, J," Josh called.

"Love you guys," Jordan said. "Let us pray."

"Ten," Simon chimed in, and then everybody else started the countdown while Jordan set the phone back in his pocket.

Nine, eight, seven, six, five, four, three, two, one…

We regret our lies, made recompense
Forgive our grave transgression
Please bring our friends back in our midst
We all have learned our lesson!

It had to be short, because there were several people reciting the spell together, but it had to be heartfelt too. As Jordan recited, he thought sincerely about the wrong of hoping some sort of magic force could fix his life, and the lengths he and his friends had gone to in order to repair what they'd done. He thought about Dante and Cully and how much he'd missed them— how much they all had missed the two men—and how he hoped they had learned the things about themselves that would make their return meaningful.

All of them had learned so much, breaking free of the ennui of abnegation and self-deprecation and leaping forward to embrace a new life, still together but changed in fundamentally positive ways.

Please, let them have learned too, he thought, even as he recited the words for the last time.

Their voices had risen and risen with each recitation, and with the final word of the final line, they could hear each other not only on the phone, but as chanting echoing off the hillsides, permeating the air. Jordan felt the cone of power first, and then he saw it, rising about their pentacle-shaped patch of land, eight colors, each one strong and noble and vulnerable and true.

That last syllable rang through the air, and Jordan and Macklin both opened themselves up to the power and allowed it to fill them.

Macklin called out, his voice vibrating with the charge of all of them, "One! Two! Three!"

And Jordan envisioned the six bonfires in his mind, as he'd seen them in the past week, as he knew they would look with their own pentagrams of sand and salt.

And then, so filled with power he couldn't breathe in, he let out a breath and lit them at the exact same time Macklin lit the candles at every site.

Fwoomph!

The fire in each site was strong—but contained. Jordan made sure it was contained. They were in fire country, and letting even a spark out of each pentagram would have been unforgivable.

He heard the combined gasps of all his friends as each bonfire site lit up, but no gasps of dismay or shrieks of "Fire! Fire!" and although he kept a tight control on his power because it was still needed, he allowed his lungs to relax and pull air in.

The next part was all him.

"Dante Francis Vianelli and Thomas Cully Cromwell, we beg you to hear our voices, our power, our call, and come to your coven, who need you!" The words were formal, and for a moment, Jordan felt a block to the power he had so easily accessed. In desperation he called, "Guys! We're right here. Get your asses out here and let us know you're all right!"

From his pocket he heard the others, probably involuntarily, begging them.

"Please, guys!"

"Cully, I miss you so much."

"Your dog needs you home!"

"Dante, man, I need you back here."

"We have so much to tell you!"

The chorus sounded almost childish, but it also sounded real and from the heart and genuine.

They missed their friends so badly.

Jordan felt tears starting, desperation and fear. Oh Goddess, oh God, oh other—what if he'd failed? What if they had made all these sacrifices and their friends were gone for good?

"I'd give everything," he whispered. "My magic, my powers, everything, just to know you were here and okay."

At a pull in his chest, Jordan thought the magic had taken him up on it. He was both destroyed and elated. He would miss it, he would, but Goddess, his friends—

And then the magic was *there*, *everywhere*, streaming from his hands, his mouth, his eyes, his *toes*, and he aimed all of it into the heart of the fire and built the bridge to the two people they'd been missing for so long.

The fire flared up, impossibly high, the flames every hue of the rainbow. Up, up, lighting the sky for miles, like an aurora borealis but more, bigger, shot through with Macklin's blue-and-gold, Jordan's sapphire, Kate's amethyst, Bartholomew's amber, Lachlan's blood jasper, Alex's emerald, Josh's aquamarine, and Simon's clear diamond. Their colors, all of them, a not-quite-complete rainbow, missing Dante's brilliant ruby and Cully's bright gold—their family, their coven, showing their colors across the sky like a beacon.

And in one breathless instant, Dante's and Cully's colors were there too.

Jordan gasped, looked back to the heart of the fire, and saw two figures emerge.

Step by step they came, lost and listing, and Jordan kept the portal built around them so they couldn't come out into harm.

One step, and then another, and then they were out of the bonfire, and then they were out of the pentagram and then they collapsed, Dante and Cully, exhausted and insensible at Jordan's feet.

Jordan gave a brief cry and doused all the bonfires in one gasp as Macklin doused all the candles, and for a moment the world was fully dark, and there existed only their harsh breaths and Dante's and Cully's soft moans.

They were fully clothed and real and clutching each other's hands.

"Jordan?"

"J?"

"Guys, you there?"

"I'm here," Jordan said, holding his sobs back with an effort. "And so are they. Guys—we did it. They're here."

He buried his face in his hands, then, and fell to his knees, barely cognizant of Macklin coming to embrace him.

"Baby," Macklin murmured, "you did it."

"We did it," Jordan said, tucking his face against Macklin's shoulder. "We all did it. We did it."

And that's as far as they got for a while.

IT took two hours to clean up, get Dante and Cully loaded into the SUV, and pretty much carried to the portable dwelling that the coven had filled with their things. They'd put the two single beds together, making a king-size, and dressed the bed that way. They figured that even if Dante and Cully weren't the couple everybody was hoping for, they would be good enough friends to need each other as the strangeness of the past month caught up with them. Bartholomew and Lachlan agreed to sleep over that night on an air mattress, in case they needed somebody to explain things, and it was just as well they took that on, because Jordan and Macklin were almost too tired to make it to their own beds.

Driving through the backroads when he was that exhausted was a surreal experience, and Jordan was grateful Macklin went first on the small unpaved dirt tracks that led from the bonfire to Dante and Cully's portable home and then from that hillside to Jordan and Macklin's.

Once they got to their own trailer, they left their vehicles in front of it willy-nilly and fell into the bed they'd hastily thrown together and made that afternoon. They were cold enough that they kept their robes on until the wee hours of the morning, when their body heat finally warmed them to the core.

They slept long past dawn.

It wasn't until Jordan awoke, sweat starting, heart pounding, as though he were late for work, school, and life all at the same time that he realized how hard—how brutally hard—waking up at dawn every morning for the past month had become.

And the lightness that permeated his heart when he realized that, for better or worse, they were done with all of that, was positively sublime.

Then he realized that Macklin was sitting up in bed, chuckling at something on his phone.

"What is it?" Jordan mumbled, trying desperately to wake up.

"My father," Macklin said, laughing. "He… he tried to find us last night."

"Find us?" Jordan sat up, alarmed, his eyes barely taking in the clean walls and skylight of this top-notch temporary home. Simon and Macklin had put some money into this venture, and Jordan could only be grateful.

"Yeah." Macklin shook his head, continuing to read. "He thought he finally figured out how to follow you after you disappeared from his property. Josue didn't help him, but Father made him watch as he summoned his own portal and disappeared around midnight. He reappeared about five minutes later, covered in fur and feathers and blood—most of it his own!"

"Blood! Oh my Goddess, is he okay?" Jordan was both appalled and, yes, a little amused. Alistair Quintero had *not* left a good impression on him.

"Well, he needed stitches and a lot of gauze," Macklin said, not nearly as concerned with his father's safety. "Apparently as soon as we retrieved your friends, the spell holding all those animals in thrall evaporated. The minute my father appeared, they all saw him and… I guess they unleashed hell!"

"Oh no!" Jordan couldn't help it—he was laughing. In his experience magic only turned on people who deserved it in ways befitting their karma.

And this sounded like karmic retribution of the purest form.

"He ripped a new portal as soon as he could and showed up in his study, raving about turkeys and squirrels from hell and crows, and he swore there were three cats there directing all the mayhem. Josue said it was *epic*. He called Billy as soon as he could this morning so he could email me the whole story." Macklin turned to Jordan with dancing eyes. "And Father swore that he'd had quite enough trouble from the two of us. He's going to leave us alone forever after this."

Jordan couldn't stop laughing. He knew that eventually he would have to get up and go get the other three familiars who had served them so well, and then he'd have to go check in on Dante and Cully and see how to help them adjust to their new situation. He'd have to see if he could transfer from the job he'd left hanging in Sacramento to a new venue in Amador County, and somewhere in there, he and Macklin would have to travel to Nevada to take care of all the remaining business there.

They weren't done with being busy by a long stretch, but now, he realized, smelling lavender and sage and sea salt and sweat on his lover's skin, there would be time. There would be time to settle in to their new lives and to celebrate the changes that had been put off for too long. There would be time to laugh with Macklin about his father's comeuppance and celebrate the apparent return of a brother.

There would be time to make love—gently, furiously, a lot—as the two of them began their lives together, with this latest quirky step forward only the first of many.

In fact, Jordan thought, kissing Macklin's neck and enjoying his hum of approval as he tilted back his head, there was time to make love *now*, on this brightest of November mornings, as the world moved toward darkness and he and his coven extended their hands to the light.

Jordan and Macklin's future stretched before them, and his future with his coven was just as bright.

A future filled with laughter, life, light, and magic.

And love. Especially filled with love.

Jordan captured Macklin's mouth and began to run his hands over a body that had become more familiar than his own.

As their bodies moved into the perennial dance, he knew this feeling, where his heart was filled with love, was the greatest magic of all.

Now Available
Shortbread and Shadows

Hedge Witches Lonely Hearts Club: Book One

When a coven of hedge witches casts a spell for their hearts' desires, the world turns upside down.

Bartholomew Baker is afraid to hope for his heart's *true* desire—the gregarious woodworker who sells his wares next to Bartholomew at the local craft fairs—so he writes the spell for his baking business to thrive and allow him to quit his office job. He'd rather pour his energy into emotionally gratifying pastry! But the magic won't allow him to lie, even to himself, and the spellcasting has unexpected consequences.

For two years Lachlan has been flirting with Bartholomew, but the shy baker with the beautiful gray eyes runs away whenever their conversation turns personal. He's about to give up hope… and then Bartholomew rushes into a convention in the midst of a spellcasting disaster of epic proportions.

Suddenly everybody wants a taste of Bartholomew's baked goods—and Bartholomew himself. Lachlan gladly jumps on for the ride, enduring rioting crowds and supernatural birds for a chance with Bartholomew. Can Bartholomew overcome the shyness that has kept him from giving his heart to Lachlan?

www.dreamspinnerpress.com

DREAMSPUN
BEYOND

Now Available
Portals and Puppy Dogs

Hedge Witches Lonely Hearts Club: Book Two

Sometimes love is flashier than magic.

On the surface, Alex Kennedy is unremarkable: average looks, boring accounting job, predictable crush on his handsome playboy boss, Simon Reddick.

But he's also a witch.

Business powerhouse Simon goes for flash and glamour… most of the time. But something about Alex makes Simon wonder what's underneath that sweet, gentle exterior.

Alex could probably dance around their attraction forever… if not for the spell gone wrong tearing apart his haunted cul-de-sac. When a portal through time and space swallows the dog he's petsitting, only for the pampered pooch to appear in the next instant on Simon's doorstep, Alex and Simon must confront not only the rogue magic trying to take over Alex's coven, but the long-buried passion they've been harboring for each other.

www.dreamspinnerpress.com